NONDESCRIPT
RAMBUNCTIOUS

NONDESCRIPT RAMBUNCTIOUS

a novel by

JACKIE BATEMAN

ANVIL
PRESS

Vancouver
2011

Anvil Press Publishers Inc.
P.O. Box 3008, Main Post Office
Vancouver, B.C. V6B 3X5 Canada
www.anvilpress.com

Library and Archives Canada Cataloguing in Publication

Bateman, Jackie, 1970-
Nondescript rambunctious / Jackie Bateman.

ISBN 978-1-897535-70-7

I. Title.

PS8603.A8385N66 2011   C813'.6   C2011-901465-3

Printed and bound in Canada
Cover and interior design by Derek von Essen
Author photo by Alfred Meikleham © 2010

Represented in Canada by the Literary Press Group
Distributed by the University of Toronto Press

The publisher gratefully acknowledges the financial assistance of the Canada Council for the Arts, the Canada Book Fund, and the Province of British Columbia through the B.C. Arts Council and the Book Publishing Tax Credit.

To Grandma Peg and the Minty Lumps

TABLE OF CONTENTS

page

CHAPTER ONE

Lauren's Blether

I had a dead brilliant day for once. It started off badly, with Jessica doing her face in the toilet to try and get out of lugging the piles of newspapers out front. Same old. The delivery van dumps these great stacks of them outside the shop before we even get to work. It's our first job to get them in the front door and put all the papers out for customers. There I was on my own, as usual, dragging them by the waxy yellow twine that held them together. It was digging into my hands something rotten. Heavy, they are. To top it all I was aching like hell, from when I gave Lizzy a backy down the road. She's getting really big now, tall for twelve, but it won't be long before she's a teenager and then she won't be seen dead having a laugh with her old mum in public. So I have to make the most of it, you know?

"Jessica, away and give us a hand, will you?"

"I'll be out in a wee minute. Okay, Lauren? I'm nearly done."

Done what, plastered on her lip-gloss for the ninety-fifth time? I knew she was waiting until I'd finished so she wouldn't have to do any dirty work and break a nail or something. She's such a skive. I left two stacks of papers outside just for her and started to cut the twine on the ones I'd brought in. The sound of the knife brought her out.

"Right, I'm ready to go. I'll start putting the papers on the shelves, then, will I?" She tottered over, everything jiggling. She wasn't wearing a bra.

"There's a couple of stacks still outside to bring in first. I kept them just for you," I said.

She scowled as she went and got them in, made a big fuss about how she could hardly move them. I just ignored her. I'm good at that. It makes me laugh, though. How the owner of the shop, Derek, doesn't lift a finger to help with things like that. It's his name on the sign outside, but we hardly even see him unless the money in the till doesn't tally up. You'd think he might at least help with the heavy lifting, but it doesn't seem to cross his mind. D. McTavish Newsagents should read Does McNothing Newsagents.

Anyway, after all the papers were put out, the regulars drifted through on their way to work, same as always. I could tell you what each of them is going to buy; they're that predictable. Even Jessica knows most of the time and she's got the brain of a flea. We've a rack in the middle of the shop, full of cards for every occasion you could think of, even one for two men getting married. There's a guy that comes in first thing, and he always buys a card, a bar of chocolate, and twenty Marlboro Reds. Always. You'd think he'd run out of people to send a card to, but not him. Then there's Mrs. Chichester from down the way, she gets the *Daily Mail* and a Passionfruit Snapple on her way to work at ScotMid. Sometimes I get a kick out of saying, "Passionfruit Snapple, is it?" or "Here's your Marlboros," and them feeling all special that I've remembered. Today it was just doing my melt in, that so many folk were stuck in a rut, so I didn't bother making an effort.

Then my day started looking up.

After the morning rush, all the oldies appeared to get their wee bags of sweeties and tobacco. Also a bit depressing, I don't mind saying. But after that, this new guy came in. I knew straight off he was from Dot Peacock's old place—we all found out that some guy had moved in a couple of weeks ago. It's a lovely wee cottage across the way, picket fence and trees all around it. One of Jessica's cousins had got a glimpse of the removal van on his way home from the pub. Apparently it came in the middle of the night. Folk have been gossiping about what he might be like because no one had seen him and he wasn't answering his door. I don't think he'd left his house until today. According to the wisest of the town, he's been a hermit with a facial disfigurement, a recluse with a humped back, a transvestite—loads of funny things that couldn't be true. Turns out he's really nice, as well as good-looking. Jessica was in the middle of texting some guy when he walked in, so luckily I got in there before she could get her dirty red fingernails on him.

"Morning, there. I'm guessing you're the one that just moved in over the road?"

"Yes, I am actually, well guessed. I'm Oliver." He came right over and looked even better close up. He was wearing gloves, though, so I couldn't see if he had a wedding ring on.

"I'm Lauren. Welcome to Dalbegie. It's not a bad place when all's said and done."

"It seems quite lovely. I think I'm going to like it here."

"So what newspaper do you read? Am I allowed to guess?" I didn't mean to prattle on at him. I'm terrible sometimes when I get talking, just can't stop.

"I read the *Times* for my sins. And no, I suppose you can't guess now, because I've just told you." He winked.

We carried on chatting for a while. He's got one of those well-to-do voices, where you can't quite tell if he's posh English or posh Scottish. Either way, he probably went to one of those schools where they play cricket and have younger boys polish their shoes. We hadn't been talking that long when Jessica interrupted us, thrusting herself in front of him like she does with all the men. I was dead annoyed. She leaned on the counter to show off her boobs and got her elbow in some black ink from the newspapers.

Serves her right. As if she doesn't get enough attention from all the single guys in town already. But he didn't give her a second look, and I think I even saw him frown, just a tiny bit. Then he carried on talking to me. It was brilliant. But did she get the hint? No, she carried on and invited him to the pub on Friday night, all casual. You should have seen her face when he turned her down. It was an absolute classic, so it was. "Thank you, but I'm busy that night," he said. He's hardly left his house all week. I think I love that man, and I don't even know him.

When I got home, I was full of the joys. Lizzy had been in from school, done her homework, and put the kettle on for a cup of tea. I could smell toast as well. I love that when I come in from work. She's so good. I can't believe my luck sometimes. She doesn't take after her rat of a father, that's for sure. I was all smiles, of course, and she wanted to know why.

"What happened to you today, Mum?"

"Nothing. I just had a good day, that's all."

"Jessica behaving herself, was she?"

"Aye, sort of." I felt guilty. Was it really that noticeable I was in a good mood? I must usually come home with a right miserable look on my face. What she must think of me. I changed the subject. "What did you get up to at school today?"

"We had a chemistry test, and Simon Travis set fire to part of the science lab."

"That boy's a numpty. I don't know why you're still friends with him."

"He's okay," she said. "It was an accident, anyway."

Aye, right. I bet the teacher didn't see it that way. We settled in, and made eggs and more toast for our tea. We used white bread like my mum used to make me when I was wee, butter running down the edges.

"Granny Mac used to make me this once a week. It was one of my best dinners."

"Mine too." Lizzy dunked a toasty finger in the egg, and yolk ran all the way down to the plate.

"Proper butter, none of that margarine muck."

"Granny Mac wouldn't have had that, right enough."

Britain's Next Top Model was on, and we sat on the sofa and watched it together, plastic trays on our laps, the salt and pepper on the fold-out table. I watched her face when they were choosing the final ten models, and she looked so young, really innocent compared to the glamorous girls on the telly. I wonder if you ever stop worrying about your kids? I can't imagine I will, not when there are boys like Simon Travis hanging around. He's trouble, that one. I know who his mum is; she goes down the social club on a Friday night with her boyfriend of the week and whoever he brings with him, usually another schemie with a mullet. She always looks like she needs to wash her hair, and smells of too much cheap perfume. Every couple of days she comes in the shop to buy Rothmans cigarettes and always looks dead rough, like she's had an all-nighter. Her husband did a runner years ago, and I reckon Simon gets left on his own a lot at night, which is why he can get away with roaming the streets in that scabby parka of his, while other kids his age are in their beds.

I looked over at Lizzy. "He's not your boyfriend, is he?"

"Who?"

"Simon Travis."

"Mum! We're just friends, that's all. I don't even want a boyfriend, for God's sake. Gross."

I left it at that. I can't stop her from talking to kids at her school now, can I? My Lizzy seems too young for boyfriends, but from what I read in the papers, you can never be too sure what goes on. Tweenies' discos and schoolgirl pregnancies and all that. Apparently they're all wearing Versace and carrying Louis Vuitton bags in London by the time they're ten years old. But I suppose they can afford that kind of thing down there. Even so, it just seems wrong.

I put Lizzy's hair in plaits before we went to bed. It makes it all wavy in the morning; it's gorgeous. That's the one good thing she got from Rob: his thick blond hair. Unlike my brown clump of a mess, all limp. Hers is the hair of an angel, I'm not kidding. We sat on her bed for a while after I'd finished. Her eyes shone as she told me all about some science project she'd been doing at school. I wasn't really listening to the details because I was that struck by her. She knew it as well, stopped partway through to give me a hug.

"Are you all right, Mum?"

"You're so beautiful, did you know that?"

"Come on, you soppy thing. Something did happen today, I can tell."

She was right, something did happen to me today, and it hasn't happened for a long time. I actually fancied someone. Since Rob left, I've hardly even thought about men, let alone looked at one. That's nearly three years of nights in front of the telly, watching my own programs at that. No footie or bloody Formula One. I do have my Fridays at the social club, mind, but that's with the girls. It's not like I'm looking for action; far from it. Every once in a while, some guy will ask if he can buy me a drink, or ask me up to dance, but none of them have interested me so far. I know most people around town, and the pickings are slim; there's an awful lot of minging men to be had. A few weeks ago, one was quite persistent, a friend of a friend who'd come to visit from Edinburgh. For some reason, he took a shine to me and kept insisting I should have a dance with him. I was having a right laugh with the girls and I didn't want to break the mood. I kept saying, "Aye, later," but he wasn't having any of it. Maggie from the café said I should just do it because he was quite nice, and I told her she should go dance with him herself. So she did. And much more as well, I heard.

"Nothing's going on, my wee angel." I kissed Lizzy on the forehead and smoothed down her duvet. "Get to sleep, you."

"Don't worry, I'll find out," she said.

CHAPTER TWO

Watch with Oliver

The cell door slammed shut behind me for the last time. I was free. The warden, Maurice, escorted me along the corridor to the stairs, everyone banging their cups along the way to say goodbye. I wasn't well liked inside, but I played the game well and had earned respect.

"Well, Oliver, good luck and keep your head down." Maurice nodded briefly and let me into the main office.

"I will, thank you, sir."

My behaviour had been impeccable, on the surface at least. I collected my belongings from the white table, including my father's watch and some loose change, and went on my way with an overwhelming sense of achievement. I'd survived and now I could resume my former life.

The truth is, my life was dominated by a dark desire. It was always there, this terrible urge to control. I felt I had been released both in body and in mind, and the prospect of unleashing my desires was unbearably exciting. When I left Inverness Prison, I walked from the cold, grey building alone. I had no home to return to, no family I could visit, and when I thought about it, I didn't have any friends either. A free man without commitment—just the way it should be.

I chose to move to Dalbegie after visiting only three other towns in the scattered network of A-roads between Inverness and Aberdeen. It was accessible only by a single-lane road and had no desirable qualities that might attract crowds, tourists, or hikers, none of which I could stand. There was no castle to photograph, nor any of those landscaped gardens that old people like to visit. "Oh, let's sit on a bench, stare into space, and drink cups of weak tea." On the other hand, it wasn't too small; it had a High Street and a sprawling mass of houses—the kind of place where I could keep a low profile. Dalbegie epitomized everything I had always liked about the Scottish Highlands. The land was wild, dotted with sharp purple thistles, the gnarled branches of the oak majestic and solid amongst the windswept chaos. There was something about the air that washed into my skin, an icy sharpness penetrating through to the core. I felt exceptionally fresh there, cleansed and ready to start living again.

Aside from the exhilarating atmosphere, the other redeeming feature about the Highlands was the affordability of property. Even with my paltry savings, I was able to buy a cottage with immaculate stonework. The place was old, but it didn't have that decrepit look about it, nothing crumbling or out of line. It faced a grassy island with iron fence-work around it—the sort of island that displayed small flowers nurtured by unseen gardeners. They fell in lines of colour, white and red with a ring of pink in the middle. It was twee and "small town," but for some reason it didn't offend me. It was home.

Before moving in, I had stipulated that any dealings would be with the estate agent alone, and that viewings would be made at unsociable hours. The sellers seemed happy enough to comply, given their desire for a quick turnaround. It wasn't long before I was moving, in the early hours of the morning of course, unloading my van swiftly in the darkness. I was used to the dark—working with it, observing in it. The town was devoid of activity, a silent place full of sleeping people. It was quite a calming experience and it didn't take me long, given that my belongings fit into eight boxes and my limited selection of furniture had already been delivered. I didn't take to clutter. When I finished, I stood in the kitchen at the front of the house as the early morning light crept into the room. Above the old porcelain sink was a window that afforded an excellent view of the local newsagents on the other side of the island. I would watch from there, and no one would know.

——◆——

For the first two weeks, I kept the curtains closed and the doors double-locked. I ate tinned food, lots of dried pasta. I didn't want to meet anyone until I was ready. The estate agent had told me that the previous owner, Mrs. Peacock, lived in the house for over forty years before she died. I was expecting some curiosity from the neighbours about who had moved in, but when someone knocked on the very first day I was shocked. Curled up on the floor next to the front door, I listened.

"The curtains are all drawn."

"Aye, but it's getting on for lunchtime. He can't be still in his bed."

"He must be out, but that van's still here. Should we try the Dalbegie Dram?"

"He'll have walked over for his first pint, right enough."

"Lovely. I just fancy a bevvy."

It seemed they already knew I was on my own. Perhaps the estate agent had spread the word somehow. I waited until the footsteps faded before I dared to move. Everything was still in boxes and I hadn't cleaned the house or even washed myself properly. It was unimaginable to meet those people, to let them in, just so they could be the first to find out my name and where I was from. What I "did." The thought sickened me.

The cottage had that universally recognizable aroma of old

lady: lavender talc, mothballs, dead skin, and rotting feet. My first task was to sanitize everything as best I could, so that her spirit would dissipate quickly. I set to work with bleach and a scrubbing brush, thankful for the lack of sunlight because seeing dust floating around made my skin crawl. I didn't need to see the dirt. The way I cleaned, there would not be a speck of filth left in the place.

Fortunately, Mrs. Peacock's family had scavenged her belongings down to the bare light bulbs, so I didn't have to deal with her tat as well as her soul. The quick "strip and sell" was beneficial to both the sellers and myself. There was a heavy wardrobe in the master bedroom, but no hope of salvaging it after too many years housing ancient polyester dresses. The stench had permeated deep into the wood, and I chopped it up for the fire. All I had to do was fumigate the place and paint the walls white to create a clean new shell.

The back garden was the best feature of my new home, with high laurels and evergreens along all sides. While the front of the house gave me access to the comings and goings of the locals, the back remained my private sanctuary. I could see out, but no one could see in. I put the firewood under the back awning and thought about what else I could hide back there.

The kitchen was my main vantage point from the front. For much of the day during those first weeks, I sat on a stool to one side of the window and enjoyed a clear view of the newsagents without being seen myself. From there, I began to get a feel for most of the people in the ragged community. I always made a point of beginning my projects slowly and methodically. If I could maintain a certain level of restraint throughout, then this one would be a success—it was all in the timing. Just once in my life, I got impatient and things went a little awry. I was determined not to make the same mistake again.

That shop. It wasn't just a newsagents; it was so much more. There appeared to be something for everyone in the place and an endless stream of people paraded in and out of it. Mrs. Peacock must have been in curtain-twitching heaven standing at my sink. I'd no doubt that she knew everyone; old people usually did. I imagined her hoisting up her sagging bra. "Oh my, look who Mr. Jones is with this morning." Well, I had one up on her. I was the proud owner of a pair of high-grade Nikon Sport Optics; the clarity was amazing. I could examine someone's shoes; see what brand they were, the colour of their soles, whether they were clean or scuffed. There was an elderly man with a white moustache who made an appearance every day at nine-thirty on the dot, and I noted that he always wore a different shirt, the collar spotless and pressed. He was sometimes accompanied by his wife, who didn't pay the same kind of attention to her appearance. More than once I saw the hem of a nightie underneath her coat.

Predictably, there was a peak time before nine in the morning, when many people bought their newspapers and cigarettes before work. Similarly, there was a busy period after five p.m., when people popped in on their way home. The retired set generally waited until after the morning rush, arriving between nine and ten, so there was a quieter time after eleven. I would pay them a visit then. One morning, I pulled on my woollen hat with the earflaps and matching gloves, and braved the open air. It was about time I made social contact; I didn't want people to think I was a total recluse. With the easy guise of buying a newspaper, I would meet the two women I had been watching. They both worked in the store most days, popping out two or three times throughout the day for breaks. One was a bottle blond and appeared younger than the other. She wore a pale shade of overly shiny lip-gloss. Her workmate was an attractive forty-something who dressed quite well. Her shoes were pristine, and she always looked clean and fresh, despite being the older model. I was immediately interested in her.

It turned out that both of them were friendly and eager to chat. The older one spoke out first and held out a tanned hand for me to shake. I hoped she didn't notice my hesitation in touching it. Her grip was a little firm for a woman, but she seemed quite feminine otherwise. She had one of those faces that look old only close up, when you can see fine lines around the eyes and clumped mascara to hide thinning eyelashes.

"So what brings you here, Oliver?"

"It's a new beginning, in a way. Family issues, you know the sort of thing," I offered vaguely. *You really don't want to know.*

"Well, there's nothing like family to make you up sticks and move." She smiled. "Mine are certainly working on me."

Meanwhile the younger girl, the bottle blond behind the counter, was texting on her mobile phone and making a revolting snorting sound through her nose. I couldn't stand people who felt the need to text, tweet, or add their mindless comments to any other pointless platform in the "social media" arena. Why anyone cared what everyone else was doing in their day-to-day mundanity was beyond me. What could she be saying? "I'm at work, snorting the contents of my nose into my gut," followed by a smiley or winking face or other such idiotic symbol. She disgusted me right from the beginning. And I couldn't stand that kind of snorted laugh; it reminded me of an old homeless person.

I tried not to look at her and concentrated instead on Lauren's smile. "I suppose you knew the previous owner of my place? More sociable than me, was she?"

"Aw, dear old Dot Peacock, we all miss her funny ways. Now there's someone who needed her family, but they only seemed to show up when there was something to be had. She lived on her own in that house for nearly twenty years. It makes me so mad when I think of it, so it does. We were all wondering if one of her revolting sons would move in, but luckily they all wanted to cash up. Not surprising, really."

She talked a lot, but the detail was only mildly irritating to me because she was so attractive. "I hope I'm a slightly better option than a revolting son."

"Oh, you'll do," she said. "Unless you have any really bad habits."

Bottle Blond sidled along the counter until she was standing opposite me and flicked back her hair in a way that said, *Look at me, I'm the pretty one.*

"I'm dead glad that you came along instead of one of them."

"Thank you. And what's your name?" *I'm asking, but I really don't care.*

"Jessica. I'm saving up to move to Glasgow, so hopefully I won't be here much longer. There's not a lot going on around here, you know what I mean?"

One of my least favourite sayings was "You know what I mean." It gave me a sudden urge to grab her by the hair, and kick it out of her.

"Well, it sounds quite good to me. I've had enough excitement recently."

"I'll be down the Dalbegie Dram Friday if you fancy meeting some folk." She flicked back her hair again; it was really starting to annoy me. Some of it stuck to the lip-gloss, and she pulled at it with chipped fingernails.

"Thank you, but I'm busy that night." *Busy thinking about your friend.*

I picked up the *Times* and handed her some change. "I'll be seeing you both again soon, no doubt." I slipped a brief wink at Lauren. She may have blushed faintly, or it could have been the light. I left and walked briskly back home before I could encounter anyone else. It wasn't good for me to meet too many new people at once, and it was pure luck that no one else came into the newsagents. The short outing had been quite a success.

Outside the house, I had touched four things. I shook Lauren's hand; held the newspaper; unintentionally touched Jessica's fingers briefly whilst giving her the money for the newspaper; and of course I opened the shop door twice. Even though I had been wearing the woollen gloves, I felt germs building up on my palms, creeping into my flesh. The pre-autumn wind had picked up outside, and the windows were creaking, irritating me. It was time for a thorough wash. I was prepared, of course, and had moved in with a substantial supply of medicated soap. Grabbing a fresh pack from the pantry, I took it straight to the bathroom, turned on the hot tap, and let it run until steam began to rise from the sink and touch my face. I liked to wash in scalding water; feel it burning the dirt from my skin, rubbing hard until I felt clean again. The soap's clinical vapour filled the room and comforted me as it always did.

When I finished, I put on a fresh pair of latex gloves so that I could read the paper without getting dirty. I bought them in bulk. They were so nice and thin; I hardly noticed I was wearing them. They could also be discarded after every use—convenient and throwaway. A bit like my women. I slumped on my new sofa and tried to read the day's news, but of course Lauren wandered into my mind; I could see her smile and the way her hair kinked out at the ends. She was an ideal candidate for my next venture, so easy to please and unassuming.

I itched to the core to plan another abduction. It was all I could think about during my spell in prison. They'd got me, but they hadn't got me for what I really did or I'd have been in there for life. Still, it had been an infuriating nine months, and now the longing was growing more intense. My cellmate, Finlay, was a gorilla, so I had kept my ideas to myself. He was from one of the more rancid parts of South London, all arms, with the confrontational stance of a Millwall supporter. Our cell smelled of a boxing-club floor that hadn't been washed in a decade. Sweat, feet, and the body odour of a thousand men were embedded in the concrete.

Over the long months of my sentence, we spent hours lying on our narrow beds, Finlay talking about his previous exploits and me pretending to listen. He insisted on having the top bunk, even though it was a struggle to hoist his lard of a body up there. His pungent feet would hang over and torment me with occasional glimpses of staticky nylon socks. The arrangement suited me in a way, despite the entire structure shaking every time he turned in his sleep. It meant I could keep my books and disinfectant wipes under my bed and I didn't have to stare at the filthy tobacco-stained ceiling covered in chewing gum. Grunting my feigned approval at his ridiculous anecdotes, I would glare at the sagging bulk above me and think of all the ways I could really shut him up.

Far worse than Finlay's drone was the whine of the simpering therapist I had to see on a weekly basis. My Friday appointment became an endurance test of sorts, an hour of utter restraint. All I wanted to do was grab her scrawny neck and squeeze it, then watch as the protruding veins bulged blue. Instead, I had to sit all placid and talk to this woman for whom I had no respect, just so that I could leave the institution with nothing further to taint my name.

Therapists like to blame everything on sex and family, so I would throw her a line. "My father died when I was very young."

She would tilt her head in sympathy and throw an equally clichéd line right back at me. "And how do you feel about that?"

"I feel angry."

"Does it feel good to say that out loud?"

"Yes, it does. It feels very good." *It would feel even better if I could throw you through that one-way mirror and watch you bleed.*
She always scribbled on a yellowing pad, curled at the edges. There were bits of flaked skin on her shoulders and stray hairs, pale ginger.

You're disgusting to me. Squeeze.

Lauren was different. I liked to look at her, listen to what she said, and I knew that her strong handshake was a façade for a weaker soul in need of attention and dominance. As with most women she would want to feel subordinate once in a while, to be passive. I was certain that I could have some fun with that one. I remembered what she had said earlier. "You'll do. Unless you have any really bad habits." It was almost as if she wanted me to have some. She had no idea.

CHAPTER THREE

Lauren's Mistakes

Sunday is the only day I don't work. It doesn't leave much time in the week for Lizzy, but we get by and how else am I supposed to make ends meet? This morning we went for a walk down the indoor market, got ourselves a punnet of strawberries, and tried on some cheap boots, the ones that come up to your knee.

"They're a bit young for me, I think." I was trying to tuck in my jeans so they didn't bag at the top, but they were the wrong kind.

"Mum, they don't look quite right." Lizzy started laughing.

"Shut it, you. Just because I can't get my arse into skinnys like you can."

"You could so."

Aye, right. I'd look like a lump, a right dafty in those. Lizzy seems to think they'd suit me, but she's obviously looking at me in a different light to most. I don't know if I'd bother trying to wedge myself into tight jeans anyway, as Oliver doesn't seem the type to like mutton dressed as lamb.

We gave the boots back to the guy that owns the stall. Paul with the Yellow Streaks, we call him between ourselves. "Maybe next time," I said. That's our code for "These are bogging."

We linked arms and giggled our way past the rest of the market sellers. They don't half have some crap in that place. Polyester tartan scarves, Caley Thistle football souvenirs, picture frames with shells stuck on them. It's amazing what people will pay good money for.

"Do you want a nice handbag with Madonna's face on it?" I picked up a plastic monstrosity and dangled it from my arm for Lizzy to see.

"Oh, thanks. That'll get me beaten up," she said.

"You being cheeky about my stock?" The guy on the stall was getting pissed off. I think he's a pal of Brian's, my brother-in-law.

"No, it's a great bag, that," said Lizzy. "It's just the wrong colour, that's all."

I put it back and pulled a face. "Maybe next time."

We had a right laugh together, then went home for lunch and a special episode of *Oprah* with Tom Cruise, what a headcase. Lizzy lay on the other end of the sofa and put her feet on my lap, and we just watched telly together with a cup of tea and packet of biscuits. It was dead nice, you know? I forgot to worry about Simon and school and her growing up, just for a while. Recently, I've been getting myself all worked up about what she's really doing after school and how often she sees that boy. When I got home from work yesterday, there was a strong smell of satsumas in the house, which made me suspicious. Lizzy was sat at the table doing her homework, which was unusual as she's usually done by that time. Her fingers were all yellow, like she'd rubbed satsuma skin all over them. I used to do that when I was young, when I'd been smoking and was trying to hide the smell.

"Still at it, are you? Do you want a hand?" I sat next to her, looked over her shoulder at her schoolbook.

"I'm nearly done. I hate geography. It's pointless."

"Well, it's good to know where you are in the world, doll."

"I know where I am. I'm right here in Scotland. I don't need to know what the capital of Venezuela is. Or how rocks got made. They're just rocks."

"Have you been smoking after school?"

"No, of course not." She didn't look at me, kept scribbling in the book.

"Were you with that Simon?"

"No, I came straight home. I've so much to do. Stop talking, will you, I'm nearly done."

I left it. No point going on, is there? I've no proof that she's smoking, and it seems silly to make such a big deal about her eating a satsuma after school. I'll just keep an eye on her to try and stop her from making the same mistakes as I did. It's blindingly obvious to me that Simon's bad news.

I know it sounds bad, and I do feel guilty about it, but I can't help but look forward to going into work tomorrow just because I'll see Oliver again. He comes in every morning now for his paper, and I really like him, I don't mind saying. For some reason, he keeps snubbing Jessica and talking to me, which is a change. There aren't many guys who would prefer me to our famous local bombshell. I can't stop wondering what his story really is, why he's in Dalbegie of all places. It's hardly a world destination.

We had a quick chat yesterday, and I got the impression he's moved away from something. Maybe he's had a bad marriage. He doesn't look much younger than me, in his late thirties or forty odd, so I wonder if he has kids? I don't like to ask; it's too obvious. I was trying to get something out of him, anything really, but it wasn't really working.

"So it's just you at the cottage, then?"

"Yes, I live alone. Just me and the *Times*." He rolled up the paper just once and put it under this arm.

"Are you a gardener? Mrs. Peacock probably has a lot of weeding left over. I don't think she could get herself out much towards the end, and her family were useless."

He paused, looked at me like I'd given him a good idea. "Yes, yes, I love the garden. Very much. And you? What do you do in your spare time?"

I thought this was leading up to him asking me out, so I blethered on about the social club and the Chinese that I like going to sometimes. He looked dead interested. His eyes never left my face and I could almost feel them burning into me. It was making me all flustered and I talked too much again. But he didn't ask me out and then I felt like a bit of an idiot. Jessica came out of the loo and then he said he had to get off, gave us one of his funny waves. We both watched as he left, pulling his hat down over his ears and thrusting his hands into his coat pockets. He's obviously not used to the cold.

"Do you think he's got someone?" Jessica filed at a hangnail and brushed the bits on the floor.

"Who knows?" I tried to sound like I didn't care. But I'm dying to know.

"I'll get him down the pub one of these days," she said.

I didn't say anything, but she'd better not. He's mine, this one.

———⊰•⊱———

The last time I had a proper crush on someone, it was when I met my ex-husband, Rob. That was a long time ago. He just ate me up, that man; I completely fell for him and his charm. If only I'd listened to Granny Mac back then, I'd have saved myself a lot of pain. I mind near the beginning we had a get-together for my sister Maureen's birthday. Everyone took loads of drink and food round to her and Brian's flat, and we all got pished together. It was before they had the kids. The party ended up being a riot. Everyone had too much to drink, there was a fight, and at least three people threw up who should have known better. I'd invited Rob and it was the first time he'd met the family and my sister's friends. I thought, well, if he can survive a party round at Maureen's place, he can get through anything. I was actually worried about him, what a joke.

In those days I still lived at home, so at the end of the night Rob walked both me and Granny Mac back together. Except in those days she wasn't Granny Mac yet, she was just my mum. We were all laughing away, trying not to stumble up the curbs or walk into lampposts. I remember being made up that Rob was having such a good time; that we were all sharing some laughs. My dad had died a couple of years back, and we really needed nights like that sometimes, to forget.

When we'd been delivered to our front door safely and Rob had sloped off, Mum went all serious. We were in the kitchen making a cup of tea and a jammy piece, and she was dead quiet. I thought she was just tired, but after she'd cut her bread into four wee squares, she held up the knife and said, "This Rob. I'm not sure about him, darling."

I sat down at the table. "You're joking. I really like him. I think I love him, Mum."

"All I'm saying is be careful. Get to know him a bit better before you rush into anything."

"He's kind and thoughtful and dead good-looking," I said. "What is it you don't like about him?"

"His eyes are too close together, and he talks to me like I'm a stupid old fool." She looked at the ceiling and slurped at her tea like she always did. She could never wait for it to cool down; had to attack it like she was in a hurry. Then she'd dunk in those Rich Tea biscuits until they were so soggy they nearly fell apart. Cheap treats are the best, she always said. Those posh ones with the chocolate in the middle didn't dunk as well.

"What exactly did he say to you? I didn't think you even talked to him much tonight."

"He came in the kitchen when I was getting myself a brandy and lemonade."

"And?"

"He helped me get the top off the bottle of lemonade and then poured it out for me."

"What's wrong with that? He was just helping you, that's just the way he is."

"It was the way he looked at me, not into my eyes but just behind me. Like I wasn't worth looking at. Then he said, "All right now, are we?" all condescending. There might be another side to him that you haven't seen yet. Just watch him, doll, that's all."

I usually listened to her. But that time I couldn't see past the rosy picture of Rob that I'd made for myself. I couldn't imagine him being rude to her. Why would he? He was brilliant and he was my man. I thought the brandy had clouded Mum's judgment that one time, and I just brushed it away. The next day Rob brought round a bunch of purple irises, just because they were my favourite. He took me for a walk in the park and held my hand, all gentle. A group of guys walked past, and he put his arm around my shoulders, protective and not a bit embarrassed at showing affection in front of them. I had thought it would always be like that, but of course it wasn't. Mum was right. I should have waited longer before I married him and I might have realized he was schizo.

I wish she were around just now to tell me what she made of Oliver. I think he'd be much too polite to speak down to any woman. I reckon she'd like him, tell me that he's a keeper. If only I could have another chance to make her proud. Granny Mac was always the voice of reason, of common sense. She was always so bloody right. Well, I think some of it finally rubbed off on me. No more mistakes. Some people say "Once a victim always a victim," but not me, not this time. If Oliver ever gets round to asking me out, he had better treat me right because if I get one sniff of trouble I'll be running a mile.

CHAPTER FOUR

Oliver Shops

My house was ready from the main floor up, but I still had to sort out the cellar. I knew it was there because the estate agent had presented me with the original drawings. It was just a question of uncovering it.

I studied the floorboards in the pantry. There was supposedly a narrow staircase leading down from there, but it was hard to see where the opening could be. The wood flooring covering the small room looked like it had been there for some years and extended through to the kitchen. On my knees, I tapped and pushed and creaked the wood until I found an area that sounded different, more hollow. I used my tools to pull up the floor in that area and found my new workspace. The steps leading down into the dark had a handrail, surprisingly solid. I leaned forward and smelled the air. Dust, emptiness, and anticipation filled my lungs. It was beautiful.

I needed some garden tools and gloves and had nearly exhausted my supply of food, so I decided to go shopping. Not ready to brave the entire community of Dalbegie in one go, I picked a supermarket with a garden centre in the nearby town of Elgin.

I had become desperate to stock up on supplies, and craved fresh fruit and vegetables to the point of dreaming about them. I also wanted to tackle the garden since Lauren asked me whether I was green fingered and I told her I was. I realized at that moment how useful the garden could be. If I began to preen and prune and build an impressive compost from the beginning, a large festering mound of soil and waste would in no way arouse suspicion later on. My garden could become an organic, environmentally friendly burial ground for all kinds of decomposing matter.

So there it was, time to get outside the house again, and the trip would get my mind off Lauren for a few hours. It made me shudder to think about all those people touching the produce, squeezing fruit to check for ripeness, or examining the underside of boxes of berries. But I was sick to death of Heinz tomato soup.

Elgin was bigger and more sprawling than Dalbegie. The supermarket was relatively clean and well laid out, but I wore my latex gloves to do the shopping regardless. They would help keep contamination at bay, at surface level anyway. When I reached the tills, I would take them off, as I didn't want anyone to notice the way I was. Not that the till girl was any kind of intelligent life form. When I finished, I unloaded my trolley in front of glazed eyes. If I was wearing a black balaclava and carrying a gun, she may not have noticed.

"It that all?" She picked at a piece of skin on her knuckle.

"Looks like it. There's nothing left on the conveyor belt."

"Want any fags?"

"No, thank you. Here's my card."

"Suit yourself."

Her grubby fingers touched mine briefly as I passed it over, and I pulled back sharply. It was a natural reaction against filth.

"What's that about?"

At least it made her look up. "I have a sore hand," I said. *If I thrust it down your throat it might feel better.*

"Some people," she muttered under her breath and rolled her eyes at the next person in the queue.

By the time I reached my car, I had touched with my bare hands the shopgirl's fingers, the plastic shopping bags, and of course the push-bar of the shopping trolley. All manner of germs must have lived on that bar alone. I struggled to stay calm for the journey back, but managed to suppress my growing rage by thinking of Lauren's face. Miraculously, it worked.

When I got home, I carefully washed all the fruit and vegetables in running water before putting them in the fridge compartments. I could almost see the germs sliding off and disappearing down the plughole. It wasn't me being overly meticulous; I knew from various scientific studies about how many forms of bacteria lie on the unwashed skin of fruit.

Once the unpacking ritual was over, I desperately needed to wash myself, but I couldn't wait any longer to see Lauren and popped over to the newsagents first. I'd had her skin, the wrinkle under her left eye, lodged in my mind and had to see the details close up again. Bottle Blonde was right there at the front, flicking her vile hair. I couldn't avoid talking to her as she was standing next to the newspapers, messing with the decrepit birthday-card stand. It was stained pale brown with years of use; I could hardly look at it without feeling nauseated. The whole place smelled of her. It was obvious that she didn't use deodorant, but simply masked her body odour with the kind of cheap body spray that can be found in a pharmacy.

"Hi there, Oliver. Come in for the *Times* again, have you?" she asked, smoothing down her tight jumper to show off her chest.

"Yes, I have, very well remembered." *For an imbecile.*

"Well, you have come in every day this week. I notice the important things, anyway." She giggled, although nothing was funny, and I had a horrible feeling she was going to snort, but thankfully she didn't. I picked up my newspaper and tried to edge away as she rambled about nothing.

Nondescript Rambunctious

"You missed a good night at the Dalbegie Dram Friday. You should come along this week. There's a crowd of us that go."

"Fridays are never any good for me. It's disappointing, but I'm bearing up," I said and moved over to the counter where Lauren had been listening.

She smiled. "That's a shame for you," she said.

"What is?"

"That you can't join in all the fun on a Friday. I never go either, because I feel like someone's granny sitting there amongst all that lot."

"You don't look your age, whatever it is." *You'd look even younger in the dim light of my cellar.*

I studied the fine lines around her eyes and decided they were quite endearing because they could only mean that she smiled a lot. I looked deep into Lauren as I said goodbye and waggled my fingers at Bottle Blonde. It was all she deserved.

I cleansed twice. Once for the supermarket experience—a whole body cleanse—then again for the newsagents, a lesser face-and-arms wash. By evening my hands were red raw, the skin split in places, blood congealing around my knuckles. I felt as though I had been released, become whole again. It was my way of controlling my mind. If I had power over my body, I could restrain myself, keep my desire from running away. I knew there was nothing worse than seeming too keen. When I met a woman with potential, a woman like Lauren, it was crucial that I distanced myself. I made the mistake of being too obvious a few years previously, when I became obsessed with a salesgirl who worked in Jenners, an old-school department store in Edinburgh.

———⊰◈⊱———

I hated Jenners. It was too big and rambling, with no defined sections. Gloves merged bizarrely into Stationery and Watches;

notelets sat in the middle of the Accessory department. The layout was backward, grotesque even, for such a supposedly high-end store. There was a musty smell too, as though I'd walked into a school that hadn't been revamped for ten generations. If I shut my eyes for a second, I was transported back to primary school and the feelings of inadequacy that plagued my life as a child. A flash of short trousers and leaky ink pens and schoolmasters. But that day it had started to rain hard and I wanted to dodge the thundercloud that was hanging over the castle and threatening an even bigger downpour on Princes Street. So I found myself darting into the store. Perhaps it wouldn't be that bad; I would buy an umbrella, then leave. However, I lost my way in the chaos of alcoves, passageways, and poor signage. That bastard of a store, it made me want to set fire to it, but as I followed the sign for Outdoor Accessories, I caught sight of my salesgirl in Bags and Wallets and calmed down. She had a presence, an air of understated confidence. Her hair was hooked behind one ear as she listened intently to what a customer was saying. She had a large frame and wore thick, flat shoes, but her manner was quite delicate. Captivated by her, I moved closer and listened to the conversation.

"And you want this bag for a wedding," she said and lightly touched her forehead, nails clean and short.

"Like I say, nothing too expensive but not cheap looking," said the customer, a middle-aged woman with stiffly sprayed hair. "And silver if you've got it. Or gold even."

"We've definitely got a couple of good options. I'll bring them over here if you'd like."

I admired the way she spoke slowly and precisely as though that customer was the most important person in the world. Never mind that she was wearing a rancid fake-fur coat and surrounded by a cloud of heavy perfume. I watched as the salesgirl, my salesgirl now, took her time picking the handbags to show the customer, examining the price tickets and putting one or two back on the shelf. I loved the way she ran her hand through her hair while she was thinking. I was hooked.

Over the next two weeks I bought three wallets, all with her help. The first was for myself and had to be black leather with a section for coins. The second was a present for my "sister" and had to be brown suede with a clasp. And the third was her choice within a budget—a present for "mother." By then I was calling her by her name, Isabelle, which was adorned on a white-and-blue name badge attached to her bosom. At the third visit, I worried that she was looking at me with a quizzical eye, but she didn't say anything to suggest she might be suspicious of my need for so many wallets. I tried to be attentive and interested in her advice, but I may have come across too intense. Then one day she saw me watching her. I thought I was hidden behind a pillar but didn't realize there was a mirror on the wall, angled so she could see me. The longer I watched her, the more I saw tragedy in her eyes, and I began to ache to get close to her, to touch her skin. I just loved a tormented woman. There were no signs that she knew I was there, but when I was asked to leave the store, it was clear she had called security. She stared at her feet when I was tapped on the shoulder by a man in uniform and continued to look down as I was being escorted out.

I called out to her while the security guard pulled at my arm. "Isabelle! I'm sorry! I didn't mean to scare you. I just thought you were beautiful."

At this she looked up at last and met my gaze with her soulful brown eyes. I believe she realized at that moment that she had lost me.

◆━◆━◆

I would never be caught watching again. Living opposite the newsagents, I could catch glimpses of Lauren in the privacy of my own home and even see her in the flesh every day if I needed to.

After all, it wasn't unusual to read a daily newspaper; no one would question that.

She could never know how much I saw of her in those first weeks. She was tired first thing; she wasn't a morning person. She walked slowly, feet dragging on the pavement, occasionally rubbing the corner of her eyes. With my binoculars, I could see freshly applied lipstick and all that dark mascara. Lauren always looked kempt at that time, regardless of how she might have been feeling. She obviously took care of herself and would never arrive at work with hair bedraggled or face unwashed. There were always tiny studs in her ears, and they were different every day. It was probably something that only she and I knew. She had both round and square silver ones; blue stones; shiny diamante; she even owned pearls. To choose a pair of earrings to wear each morning had obviously given her such pleasure. I wondered if there was an anguished story behind any of them and longed to know it.

Patience. Wait for the right time.

At lunchtime, the two girls always went out separately, Lauren at twelve-thirty and then Jessica at one-thirty. Jessica squandered most of her hour, wandering aimlessly around the outside of the fenced flowerbed, smoking one cigarette after the other. Occasionally, she met a man she knew and flirted for a while. I found she had a penchant for men with motorbikes, much to my disgust. Oily fingers and tight leather, a breeding ground for bacteria. It was just another trait that made her more repugnant. But Lauren made the most of her time alone, and often took a book to Stone's Café around the corner. It was a tiny place with wooden tables and tea presented in large china mugs. I followed her there many times. If I walked on the opposite side of the road, I could see her sitting in the window, concentrating on her book while she ate her lunch. It was never too busy in there during the week, and she seemed to really enjoy the solitude. She consumed romantic novels at a rapid pace. They weren't the racy Hollywood kind, but the old-fashioned

Nondescript Rambunctious

whimsical stories, with knights on horseback or swans in a lake on their covers. A small-town woman lost in an idealized world. In real life, she only met men like me.

One day I walked past and she looked up, as though she could sense me. I had been trying to see what she was eating and was straining my neck slightly. I was afraid it was obvious that I was looking and tried to seem casual about it, gave her a wave and a smile without changing my pace. She smiled back and then dropped into her book again. One day soon she would belong to me, become a part of my secret world. And in some small way, I knew she would enjoy it.

CHAPTER FIVE

Lizzy at the River

I started to think Mum was in love. I could see it in her face; she was away with the fairies most of the time, and she kept smiling at nothing. I'd never seen her like that. She kept on looking at me all dreamy and said loads of soppy things. It was like she'd never really looked at me properly before. Suddenly she was noticing my hair and got all interested in what I'd been up to at school. Weird, so it was. Molly agreed with me that my dear mother had lost the plot or there was some guy in the running.

I'd seen it all before with some of the older girls at school. Like that Cassandra McVey in the year above me. She just sat about and doodled some guy's name on her pencil case all day. I didn't know who the guy was, but knowing her, it was probably just someone in a boy band she was never going to meet. It was like once you hit thirteen, you became some kind of mental case. There was another girl in the year above, Sarah something or other, who didn't eat. Ever. She was all bones and baggy jumpers, and all she had—all day—was water and one Cup-a-Soup. It was mad. Molly and me made a pact. When we got to thirteen, we'd have a right go at each other if we got stupid. She was going to call it if I started mooning around, scratching my arms with a razor blade and not eating chips, and vice versa. We'd look out for each other, and fingers crossed, keep from turning into head cases.

It wasn't like Mum was a teenager anymore, though; far from it. She was quite old compared to some of the other mums, really. Maybe if you fell in love when you were old, all the symptoms of being thirteen came back and you became a mental again. That was the only thing I could think of because Mum was definitely not stupid like Cassandra McVey and wouldn't normally be all drippy like that either. It was worrying, right enough, because who the hell was she in love with and what was he like? If Dad was anything to go by, she wasn't that great at picking men.

I loved my dad, sort of, but he was violent. Not to me, but he hit my mum on and off for about ten years before she told him to get lost. So for the last three years, I'd only seen him once a year at Christmas and even that upset her. I liked seeing him because he was my dad, but if I was honest, I didn't really mind that it was only once a year. He bought me some good presents because he felt so guilty that he wasn't around. I still felt a bit scared around him, like he was going to explode any minute.

I used to sit on the stair and listen to their arguments; they were bad, dead scary. One night, just before he left for good, they were shouting so loud and things were smashing on the walls, so I ran away to Molly's for the night. I was so scared that Dad was going to come upstairs and throw things at me as well. I put my clothes on and tiptoed down the stair, no problem. They were being too noisy to notice. Molly stayed just down the road so it wasn't far to go. I chucked a stone at her bedroom window and she let me in. I got into trouble for it, but in the end it was her dad, not mine, that got angry. When he found out I was in her room the next morning, he was dead angry and stood there in the doorway with his hands on his hips, bright red.

"What are you doing here, lassie?"

"I ran away last night. I was feared."

"Feared of what? You're nine years old. What are you doing out on your own at night? You should be at home. Your mum will be worrying herself sick." He ranted away while we stared up át him from the edge of the bed.

"They were breaking everything in the house."

"Eh?"

Molly piped up. "Dad, can Lizzy stay with us?"

He'd heard me but answered Molly instead. "She needs to get back home. Don't be ridiculous. Get up, Lizzy, and I'll take you back right now."

He went downstairs, and I could hear him going off to Molly's mum that I was round there, that I was a wee besom and should be told. Apparently, I was a bad influence, too; that was a joke. It was Molly that was the naughty one in those days.

I got up and rubbed my eyes, already dressed in the clothes I had pulled on the night before. Molly shrugged and said she was sorry that I couldn't stay. There wasn't much we could do about it though; that was the frustrating thing about being a kid.

She hugged me. "Good luck, Lizzy. Don't let him touch you, okay?"

"If he tries anything, I'm running straight back here, don't worry."

When we got to my house, I felt dead nervous and dreaded my dad coming to the door. But it was Mum that answered. She was still in her dressing gown, and Molly's dad took a step back, nearly knocked into me. Mum's face was half-covered with a scarf, but you could tell it was bruised and all swollen. Her skin was red and blotchy, which was what happened when she cried.

"Christ, are you okay, Lauren?"

"I'm fine. What's this? Did Lizzy end up at your place?"

"She stayed the night with Molly. Did you not notice she was gone?"

"I thought she was in her bed." Mum's eyes filled up.

"Lauren, call us if you need anything, okay? Cheerio, wee thing." Molly's dad touched my shoulder and then left, his head shaking like he couldn't believe it.

Nondescript Rambunctious

I reckon he knew what was going on. But no one says anything, do they? I gave Mum a cuddle. She cried, lifted me up like I was a baby and I could feel her tears all wet on the back of my neck.

"Where's Dad?"

"He's gone away to his brother's for a couple of nights, my love."

"I think he should stay there a bit longer than just two nights, Mum."

"Maybe you're right," she said and held me so tight I could hardly breathe.

⁌⸱⸱⸱⸱⁌

If Mum was in love again, I hoped it was with someone nice. With money and maybe a Wii. We couldn't afford one of them. Some great guy who always looked out for people, especially people's daughters. I didn't really care what he looked like because everyone says it's what's on the inside that counts, and I agree with that, honest I do. I would have been happy with someone that didn't have a heavy hand, simple as that. Mum couldn't handle any crap, not again.

There was no way I was going to get all stupid over Simon Travis, even though I really liked him. I knew what everyone else thought of him, as well. A lot of folk said he was a ned and a waster because of his mum and because he was bad at school. But he wasn't like that when you got to know him. Molly said there was some talk about what was going on between him and me, but there was nothing funny happening. He was just a friend and a good one as well. Molly got jealous when I hung out with Simon at break or after school. We'd been best friends since we were in Primary One, and she got a bit needy when I got pally with anyone else. That was just her, though; the way she was.

I could get away with seeing Simon after school because Mum didn't get in from work until after six. She thought I went straight home, but most days I ran up to the river with him, and we sat and talked and threw sticks into the water. Sometimes he brought a flask of whisky with him that he'd taken from his mum's stash, and we sipped it until it made us all giggly. He was dead funny and did impressions of all our teachers. We had this chemistry teacher, Mrs. Gregory, who wheezed between sentences because she only had one lung. He went off about making crystals and the colour of Bunsen burner flames and sounded just like her; it had me in pieces. He also did a good Mr. Johnston, the PE teacher, who was a bit camp and wore tight trousers. It was pure mad.

One time when we were down at the river, I thought he was actually going to cry, I really did. It was getting really cold out and he'd got some whisky and that warmed us up a bit. He wasn't himself, seemed a bit down—when I asked him what was wrong, he went off on one.

"It's my mum. She's with that choob Dave Wilkie again. I can't stand him; he's obviously on something all the time. His eyes are always spaced out, and he looks like he's out for what he can get all the time."

"What's she with him again for?"

"I don't know," he said. "I think she gets desperate."

"Does he stay round at yours then?"

He nodded and took a swig of whisky although it seemed like he'd had enough by then. I didn't really know what to say because I thought his mum was a bit of a slapper and I knew a lot of other people did too. She went from one guy to the next without blinking.

"He won't last long," I said.

"What's that supposed to mean?"

"I didn't mean anything. Just that he won't be around for long; they never are, those sorts of guys. You'll be rid of him soon enough, don't worry."

"Well, he's been around before and he's around again now," he said and took another swig.

I felt bad for him, but I didn't know what to say, not when it was his own mum that was putting it about like that. I didn't really know Dave Wilkie, but I'd seen him out and about and he looked dodgy. He had one of those tattoos that looked like he did it himself with a Biro.

"Does he say anything to you? When he's round at yours?"

"Not much," he said. "Mostly he wants me out of the house, so he gives me some money and tells me to get lost."

"What does your mum say?

"She's out of it most of the time, so she doesn't say anything; just lets him get what he wants. She wouldn't notice if I just disappeared, honest she wouldn't. Not if she had enough voddy in her."

"That's not true," I said, even though it probably was true. "It'll all get better again, you'll see."

He shrugged and finished off the whisky. He hadn't been that serious before, usually we just mucked about. It might have been the drink, but I saw a different Simon that day. He was a wee soul, so he was. I asked him if he wanted to come back to ours for something to eat, but he said he had to get going. He looked like he could do with a good feed sometimes; I bet his mum didn't ever cook his tea for him. More like he had to get some chips or something with the money that her ned pen-tattoo boyfriend gave him.

I was sorry he didn't come over because I thought if Mum met Simon properly she wouldn't mind me hanging out with him so much. She'd be able to see for herself that he was all right, a good guy. She could stop worrying about me then and concentrate on her new man, whoever he was. Granny Mac used to say my mum was a Willy Worry and that even when she was a wee girl, she would fret about everything. There was some story about Mum when she was three years old. She was always going on about a homeless guy that lived under a bench in town. She waved to him every day when Granny Mac used to take her to nursery, and one day she took him a current bun for his elevenses. Now she had thick lines on her forehead, and I was sure they were from all the worrying she'd done over the years.

That day, after Simon nearly cried at the river, I brushed my teeth and ate an orange to get rid of the smell of whisky, then put the kettle on for tea. I could usually time it just right, so that it boiled when Mum walked in the door from work. She kicked off her shoes and sat down at the kitchen table with this funny smile on her face.

"I'm that desperate for a cup of tea. You have no idea. You're my wee angel, so you are," she said.

"Did Jessica skive off all the jobs today again?"

"Aye, no more than usual, mind. You'd think I'd be used to it by now."

"See your boyfriend today, did you, Mum?"

"Are you joking? No way, I haven't met some guy. I'm not ready for all of that nonsense," she said and laughed. She got up from the table and pulled her hair-tie off and messed up her hair. Usually she sat down and drank her tea with me at the table for a bit, but she went off to her room, said she wanted to have a bath before we had our dinner. Said she was exhausted from lugging all the papers and a new delivery of sweeties around the shop. She wasn't looking me in the eye when she told me all of this, and then I was even more convinced there was a guy on the way. I decided I'd do a bit of spying with Molly; she was dead good at it. It would give her something to do and distract her from being jealous of Simon as well. I'd soon find out what was going on; you couldn't hide much from anyone in Dalbegie. There was always somebody that knew something, which was the good thing and also the bad thing about it. You could hide, but not for long.

CHAPTER SIX

Lauren and the Dried Leaves

This is all starting to drive me a wee bit nuts. Oliver has been in the shop just about every day since I met him, and I'm getting nowhere with him. He's always in and out of the place like he's in a big rush. I know he likes me, because he always ignores all of Jessica's blether and winks and makes a point of talking to me. That sounds daft, but you know, you can tell when someone likes you. He looks at me really intensely and smiles and his eyes sparkle. But then again we have this three-minute conversation about nothing and then he leaves. I'm just left there with the smell of him, wishing he could have stayed longer.

It's difficult when you're in a shop because there's always someone else around listening to your chat, even if it's just Jessica. Well, especially if it's just Jessica because she always tries to join in if she hasn't got any other customers to flirt with, and it's dead annoying. It must be four weeks or something by now since Oliver moved here, and I don't really know anything about him other than that he lives over the road, reads the *Times*, and washes with something strong that I can't quite place. I hardly ever see him about the town either, and when I do, he's just walking past the café or somewhere in a hurry again.

So I've decided that if he asks me out, he asks me out. And

if he doesn't, he doesn't. I'm not going to make a fool of myself by being obvious like Jessica does. There's nothing I can do but smile and wait. In the meantime, I'm going to keep myself busy by helping Maureen out a bit more. With four kids and a useless husband, she needs all the help she can get, and that's what sisters are for, I suppose. Noah hasn't even reached his first birthday yet, and I know how difficult it is to look after a baby, let alone with another three wee ones. How anyone can be unlucky enough to get four boys, I don't know. You might as well throw out your address book because there's nobody that wants to be around you with that houseful. Billy, Kai, Kane, and baby Noah. No prizes for guessing who came up with those names—Brian chose Billy after his dad, then Maureen had free rein after that. She was always one to be different. I popped round in the afternoon with a smile on my face just for her.

"Lauren, thank God!" she shouted at me as she opened her front door. The scarf on her head wasn't a good look, not with her nose. It looked like she had alopecia or something and needed to cover it up.

"I've got rubber gloves in my bag. What do you want me to do?"

"Bless you. Get in here and get that kettle on, for starters."

Baby Noah had filled his nappy, and there was a bit of a smell in the front room, I don't mind saying. Maureen said she hadn't had time to change him yet because the twins, Kai and Kane, had been trying to empty her kitchen cupboards and she'd been busy trying to stop them. They call that age the terrible twos; since there are two of them, I don't know what that makes. Terrible fours in their case, I reckon. Billy was at a friend's house having his tea, so that was one less worry, although he was due back at six-thirty. He just started school this year, and he's started to have tea at his pal's sometimes, which helps. So grown up. When I see him with his wee satchel, I could cry.

Maureen gave me one of those looks that said, "Can you please take over?" So I did.

"Kai! Kane! Give it a rest, will you!"

Kane looked up at me and smiled, all sweetness, then opened another cupboard door. I grabbed his arm and took hold of Kai's hand and pulled them into the front room.

"I'll make you some dinner if you like, my wee darlings," I said and put the telly on. It was already set to a cartoon channel, so I just turned up the sound and popped them on the sofa together. They're two peas in a pod, they are. I don't know who they look like, not any of our side of the family that's for sure. Blond hair and pale skin, they must take after someone on Brian's side. I grabbed a sponge to wipe up the biscuit crushed into the sofa cushions.

"Maureen! What will I make for their tea?"

"Have a look in the cupboard. There should be a tin of beans or spaghetti hoops or something," she shouted down from the bedroom where she was changing Noah. "There's bread in the freezer."

I don't know how they get on for money, I really don't. Brian has to work a lot of shifts at the factory, that's for sure. It's a wonder they see each other at all. He might be useless around the house and a bit of a drip, but he's a hard worker right enough. I kicked myself that I hadn't taken anything round, even a packet of minirolls from the shop. Next time. I put four slices of bread in the toaster and fished around the mess for a tin opener.

Maureen appeared with Noah under one arm. "And how are you getting on? Are you feeling all right?"

"I'm fine. There's nothing wrong with me."

"You look well, Lauren. Best I've seen you in a while, I have to say. Less pale."

"Thanks a lot."

Ever since my face had its last fight with Rob's fists, I've been having dizzy spells and my left ear still makes a ringing noise after all this time. I was checked out at the hospital straight after it happened and was told that it looked worse than it was because of the terrible bruising around my eyes and nose. I could hardly see out of one eye because it closed up so much. I wouldn't let Lizzy see me in the hospital and had Maureen watch her for a few days until the swellings went down a bit. They kept me in for a couple of nights to make sure my head was all right as I'd been knocked out for a while. I remember feeling like the elephant man or something; my face was so big. But the test proved fine, and they let me go home as long as I agreed to see a social worker the next day. But all that was a fair while ago now.

"You'd tell me, wouldn't you, if you were getting dizzy again?" Maureen asked.

"Of course," I lied. "You don't have to worry about me. You've enough on your plate."

"What about the sounds in your ear?"

"Not for ages, honest. Kai! Kane! Get in here for your tea!"

The boys ignored me, and I had to go and drag them into the kitchen. Maureen sat down at the kitchen table to feed Noah and sighed. She always looks like she hasn't slept in a week, so she does.

"And you're still okay on your own? There's nothing you want Brian to do for you around the house?"

I tried not to laugh at the thought of Brian coming round to fix something. I'd be surprised if he even has any tools. "No, away with you. I'm fine. I love being on my own. And I've got Lizzy don't forget. She's a wee angel."

Maureen feels sorry for me because I'm on my own, a victim of abuse from my ex-husband with no sign of another man on the horizon. To her, being married is the answer to everything. She wanted to get married right from when she was a wee girl; I remember her favourite dressing-up outfit was that white dress with the tiara. She used to look at herself in the mirror and pretend she was getting ready for her big day. I'm three years older and used to be the bridesmaid. And if I didn't want to be a bridesmaid, I'd be a cowboy and run around shooting the walls with a potato gun.

When she got older, she used to write down a boy's name next to hers and work out what their children's names would be if they got married. The boy's name would change every so often depending on who she fancied at the time. I can't remember how she did it, but she would cross out letters and add some numbers up and then come up with some theory. It's funny how some girls are like that, all geared up for marriage from the minute they're born. The next minute, they're up to their necks in kids and useless husbands and wondering where their lives went.

"I'll give the kids their bath if you like, and put them in their beds. I can come round once a week and give you a break. What do you think?"

Maureen looked like she was going to burst into tears. "That would be great. Brian's working late at the moment, and it's a long day, you know?"

"I know. It's no problem. Lizzy gets on with her homework after school, and she won't mind if I'm back a bit later sometimes. I can get carry-out for the both of us on the way home," I said.

"Thanks, Lauren. I mean it."

I waved her away and took Noah from her arms. "Come on, wee man; let's get you sorted. Kai and Kane, let's get up the stairs if you've finished your beans. You're a wee pair of mucky mucksters."

I turned as I went up the stair after them and saw Maureen slump into an armchair. She closed her eyes and looked like she was going to fall asleep. Bless her, she looked so peaceful, even if it was just for a minute. I'd like to say Brian appreciates everything she does, but a big part of me knows he doesn't have a clue. That's just life.

⇒•⇐

When I finally left Maureen's and took the short walk home, it was later than I thought. I stopped at the chippy and picked up two fish suppers for tea. The owner, Jack, was frying the fish, and his son Jonno was serving them up. Jonno doesn't usually work. He's not the full shilling and often just sits and reads science books, so it was nice to see him at the counter for a change. He always gives me a lovely smile. Anyway, the smell of the fish suppers under my arm was making my mouth water, and Lizzy was looking out of the kitchen window for me like she could smell them from there. I waved and she let me in the front door, looking at me expectantly.

"Sorry, I should have given you a call," I said. "I was over at Maureen's and the time just went. She was that tired, I ended up putting the boys to bed for her."

"Are you sure you were at Auntie Maureen's?"

"Of course. What do you mean?"

"Nothing," she said and put the kettle on. There were some dried leaves in the back of her hair, like she'd been lying on the ground. I pulled at them and asked her what she'd been doing.

"Some boys were chucking leaves at us in the playground, that's all," she said but didn't look at me.

"What boys were they? Simon Travis?"

"Why have you got a thing about Simon Travis?"

"I don't want you hanging around with him; he's bad news. You know what I think of him and his skanky mother."

"It's not his fault he's got a skanky mother," she said.

She's right. It isn't his fault, but it doesn't mean I trust him as far as I could throw him. I saw him the other day in the street, and he looked like he'd been drinking or worse. He skulks along, looking at the pavement, holding a cigarette in the palm of his hand like an old man. He probably reeks of smoke when he gets home, but his ma wouldn't notice or even care if she did. I chucked a couple of plates and forks on the table and grabbed the fish suppers. "In the paper or out?"

"Let's keep them in the paper. They taste better like that," she said and sat down with me. She seems so young sometimes; it scares me to think she's started secondary school already.

"Just be careful, darling," I said and picked the last leaf out of her hair.

"Of what?"

"You know what I mean."

CHAPTER SEVEN

Oliver's Dinner

She was almost eating out of my hand and all because I didn't try too hard. Life was funny that way. If only I'd known that kind of restraint when I was younger. I would have had so much more success with women. Instead I was persistent, downright pushy, and scared away most of my potentials in those days. Isabelle in Jenners department store was just one of a few disasters.

Lauren and I went out for Chinese food. It was our first night out after a few weeks of light conversation and insinuation, between interruptions by our friend in the tight jumpers. When I asked her out, she just stared at me, and for one horrible moment, I thought I'd misread the whole situation. But she gushed her approval, as long as we avoided the Dalbegie Dram where Jessica and the younger crowd drank. Of course that suited me well. We also avoided the social club where Lauren usually met her friends on Friday. She maintained that Friday nights at the Bright Pearl were relatively quiet, until closing time at least. Keeping our meeting private suited me perfectly. Apart from the fact that I was a hopeless small talker in a crowd, the less people that knew about our growing relationship, the better. Secrets like that were a godsend for someone like me.

I felt anxious at the thought of eating food made by strangers, something I rarely did. Even using cutlery from an unknown kitchen made me shiver with disgust. I resolved to drink from previously unopened bottles, eat little, and hoped that I wouldn't begin to sweat during the meal. The effort would be worth it.

Lauren met me at the restaurant because she didn't want me to pick her up and for her daughter to see us together. More secrets. I was punctual as always and waiting for her at the table when she arrived. I had ordered a good Sancerre and some bottled sparkling water, and she seemed pleasantly surprised that I had done so, that I had taken charge. When I stood up and pulled back her chair, she flushed slightly and took some time removing her coat before she sat down. I gave it to the waiter to hang up and poured out the wine myself.

"Well, cheers, Oliver." She touched her glass against mine.

"Here's to a fresh start."

"Is that a fresh start in general or a fresh start with me?"

"Both," I said.

She was bold; I liked that. We looked through the menu and fortunately she didn't suggest we share a selection of food. When people swapped spoons and grabbed and spilled in their eagerness to get a taste of everything, it spoiled my appetite.

"I'm going to have the spring rolls followed by the beef chow mein," I offered.

"I'll have the healthy option. Hot and sour soup, then the prawn stir-fry," she said and put her menu firmly back on the table.

Things were going well already. I studied her hair, freshly washed and shining with a product that smelled like almonds. She took good care of her appearance. Her nails were very clean and cut short, nice and clear, not painted some ghastly colour. The lighting in the restaurant was flattering to her face as well; they had presumably set it at a low level to hide the flaws in the wallpaper and the nicotine stains on the ceiling.

"What perfume are you wearing?"

"It's Chanel No. 5," she said. "An old classic that my mum used to wear. It's kind of stuck with me. Like it?"

"I do. As you say, it's classic. It suits you."

She didn't usually wear perfume; in the shop she smelled of newsprint and spearmint chewing gum as well as her almond shampoo. She must have dabbed on the Chanel especially for our night out, which was a good sign. We had a pleasant evening and talked without any embarrassing silences while we drank the bottle of wine plus two more glasses. What little food I ate was average, but the wine was surprisingly good for a low-key restaurant in a small town. I managed to steer away from talking about my past for most of the evening, and we discussed her family and the trials and tribulations of having a daughter who is about to enter her teenage years. As with most women, she loved talking about people, and I got a detailed description of her sister and why she was helping out with her sons.

I hoped I looked interested. While she spoke, I tried to focus my eyes on hers rather than on other parts of her anatomy that I would like to see in the flesh. Her neck was quite fragile, long and slim and surprisingly free of lines given her age. I imagined I could put my hands around it and easily fold my fingers together at the back.

By the time were sipping at our extra glasses of wine, Lauren was quizzing me about my family and why I had appeared in Dalbegie of all places. I told her that my parents were no longer alive and that I was an only child. Easy.

"What about other family?" she persisted.

"I have elderly aunts and uncles, but they all live in the south of England and I have little contact with them," I said.

"Whereabouts in the south?"

"My mother was from Dorset and my father from Cornwall, but we didn't live there when I was a child. We lived in North London and then Edinburgh. So really I have no close family, and many of my friends are scattered around the world these days."

Nondescript Rambunctious

"So you've no one really?" She actually looked worried about me.

"I suppose not. Not here, anyway. But then again I don't need anyone to look out for me anymore." *It's you that needs looking out for, my dear.*

"You still haven't told me why you've moved here," she said. "Who are you making a fresh start from?"

She looked a little anxious, and it occurred to me that she might have thought I was divorced or separated. Most men of my age were married or had been married before. She certainly gave me the perfect reason to be somewhere new without raising suspicion. So I went along with it and fabricated an ex-wife. It was astounding that I hadn't thought of it before.

"It's a fresh start from my past," I said. "My past who went from sweet, innocent bride to demonic nutter in the space of about five years."

She laughed and took another gulp of wine. She was getting quite tipsy, and I was tempted to ask her back to the house that very night. But I hadn't got everything quite ready, in perfect order, just how I liked it. Not the right time.

"No kids, then?"

"No kids," I said. "Which was part of the problem I think. She didn't have anyone to think about aside from herself."

"That's a common problem, right enough."

I was proud of myself. In the space of a few minutes, I had established a no-ties family, a reason for being there, and the perception that I had previously led a normal marital life that had ended through no fault of my own. I had been waiting for her to ask me what I did for a living and thought perhaps I had got away with it. But of course the dreaded question came next. Luckily I had rehearsed that answer.

"So what do you do with yourself, Oliver?"

"I'm a freelance writer. I work at home and rarely have to meet face to face with clients, so I can live anywhere. I write for websites, knowledge-based ones mainly. It's laborious and doesn't require much inspiration, but it pays the bills," I said.

"No romantic novels, then?"

"I'm afraid not. But I could give it a go in my spare time." *As long as they included something "extra."*

"Maybe not, eh. But I get why you stay in your house so much. You'll be concentrating on all that writing."

"Yes, yes, I need a lot of quiet. Sorry if I seemed a little reclusive at first."

"No, away with you. Of course not."

I paid the bill and insisted that I walk her home. She lived on Bryant Road just fifteen minutes' walk away, and I persuaded her that it was no trouble. She was reluctant to be seen with me because she said her daughter often looked out the window for her, so we agreed that I should walk her most of the way down her road but stay out of sight. It was earlier than it would have been if she'd gone to her social club, so there wasn't much chance of being looked out for, but she said better to be safe.

"I've had a lovely evening; thank you for dinner." She touched my arm lightly. A bolt went through me. I hadn't been touched like that by a woman for a long time.

"You are welcome; it was absolutely my pleasure. I would like to take you out again next week if you're free."

"I'll have to check my diary, but I'm pretty sure I'm free most nights," she laughed.

"That's if Billy, Kai, and Kane don't need you." I had made sure I remembered their names. "And Noah, of course." Women love that kind of thing.

We walked slowly although it was a cold night, frost already covering the roads. The grey brick buildings looked black in the dim glow of the streetlights. I offered her my coat, but she insisted she was fine wearing her thin black jacket. It was quiet. Most people who had ventured out were still in the warmth of the pubs, basking

Nondescript Rambunctious

in the smell of beer and incessant chatter. The sharp heels of her boots made a clicking sound that echoed along the street, and I imagined her unzipping them slowly and throwing them on the floor when she got home.

She stopped and turned to me. I blinked, brought myself back to reality.

"Well, this is me. I live at number twenty over there, so I'll be fine now."

"Goodnight, Lauren." I quickly turned away before I did something rash. I walked to the end of the road without looking back. I liked to be absolutely ready when I made my moves.

I touched so many public objects that evening, it hurt my head to think of them all. My hands were shaking and tingling when I took my front door key out of my pocket and then I could hardly turn the lock. There was the well-used door of the restaurant; the chairs, both mine and hers; the menus that hundreds of customers must have pored over with their dirty fingers; cutlery previously set out by wait staff; the wine bottle and glasses. Contamination seeped into my pores, itched at my insides. I had to wash the instant I set foot in the door. I ran to the bathroom and peeled off my clothes, thick with filth. Taking the soap and the scrubbing brush into the shower, I turned it on as hot as it would go and stood under the scalding water until I could feel it burn my scalp. Steam filled the room as I washed and scrubbed over and over until I was free again.

When I left the house the next morning to go to the newsagents, I had to put on a woollen hat to hide the pink burn marks on my head. They weren't too bad and would disappear within a couple of days, but I didn't want to draw attention to myself. Lauren would also wonder what had happened, particularly as she'd only just seen me the night before. She always worked on a Saturday morning then had the rest of the weekend off, so I knew she would be in the shop.

Predictably, Bottle Blond tried to commandeer me as soon as I went inside. She was wearing tight jeans and an inappropriately low-cut top given the weather. Jeans always made me cringe because people wear them for days on end without washing them. It's a fact. Denim gets uncomfortable straight after laundering, and for that reason people don't wash them often enough. This is particularly true of tight jeans.

"Good morning, Oliver." She flicked her hair.

"What a chilly day it is so far," I replied and looked pointedly at her top. I saw Lauren smile.

"What are you up to this weekend?"

"This and that. I have some work to catch up on." I grabbed the *Times* as fast as I could.

"Get up to much last night?" I asked Lauren as she rang in my purchase.

"Quiet night in. Cup of cocoa," she said with a glint in her eye.

"Same here."

If Jessica knew we had spent the evening together, she might have stopped thrusting out her bosom and flirting in such an overtly painful way. But perhaps that was wishful thinking.

"Bye, Oliver. See you on Monday," she called after me as I left the shop.

I gave her a dismissive wave. "Look forward to it!"

I went straight to Bryant Road and walked past number twenty. It was a small, semi-detached brick house with a green front door and potted plants around the porch. It looked exactly like the kind of place I imagined Lauren living in. Neat and tidy, small and homely. Only two of them lived there, her and the daughter Lizzy, so there must have been plenty of room. Just as I was wondering if her daughter looked anything like her, I heard a front door slam behind me and a young girl skipped out of the house. I turned to look briefly and saw that she was blond, skinny, and waif-like. Not like her mother at all. Another young girl appeared farther down the road and called out to her.

"Lizzy! Are you ready then? Let's go!"

So it was definitely the daughter. I reached the end of the road and hoped no one was watching as I turned back on myself and walked in their direction. The two girls were turning left at the other end and I quickened my pace to lessen the distance between us so that I could follow them. They walked down to the High Street and stopped in the fish and chip shop. They came out sharing a bag of chips, the smell of salt and vinegar wafting back at me, almost making me hungry. Not that I would have eaten food from a soggy bag wrapped in a filthy newspaper. The friend ate more than Lizzy and crammed the last few chips in her mouth before screwing up the paper and throwing it into a street bin. She had a stockier build and was wearing a thick down jacket that made her body look square.

They made their way down to Dave's Discs, the local music store, and stayed in there for around thirty minutes. There was only so long that a man could hang around one part of the small High Street without being conspicuous, and I was about to leave when they came back out, each carrying a plastic bag with the DD logo on it. They hugged briefly, and I could just about hear them speak from where I was standing, pretending to look in the window of a hardware store.

"So, I'll see you tomorrow then?" said the friend.

"Aye, come over tomorrow afternoon and we'll play the CDs.

I'm having lunch at my Auntie Maureen's, but we'll be finished by two because that's about as long as she can take having visitors over." Lizzy kicked at the edge of the curb, scuffing her shoe.

"Your mum won't mind then?"

"No, she's in a world of her own at the moment."

They parted company, and Lizzy walked purposefully towards the riverbank, her friend dithering for a moment before wandering off in the opposite direction. I had no interest in her friend, so I waited for a few moments before following Lizzy. I had her alone, which might have turned interesting. She reached the water and walked along the pathway next to it, finding her way at the edge to avoid the wet mud that had been accumulating over the past couple of weeks. The river had swollen and changed colour from blue to grey in those dark days, a contrast to the bright orange and yellow leaves that had fallen into its waters, swirling around with the currents. I was thankful for the woollen hat then, even the sounds of the ice-cold water making me chilled. After only twenty yards or so, she waved and quickened her pace. A young boy shouted with the gravelly tone of a newly broken voice.

"Lizzy! Can you climb up here? It's a great spot."

"I'll try," she shouted back.

"If not, I'll come back down. Don't worry yourself."

She clambered up the steep bank to where the voice was coming from. I couldn't see him as I was standing behind some tall shrubbery, not wanting to risk being seen myself. I crept closer but couldn't hear them over the sounds of the churning water. The smell of cigarette smoke drifted over. So she had a male friend. Lizzy clearly wasn't too young to have a boyfriend. I knew her mother thought otherwise.

So that day ended up being good for information gathering. No details were irrelevant, no matter how trivial. The most interesting facts were that Lizzy appeared to have a regular meeting place with her male friend in a relatively desolate place. And she was alone

Nondescript Rambunctious

for a short time before she met him, which was worth keeping in mind. But first I wanted to concentrate on her mother, who was keen, malleable, and a little bit desperate. And I needed to move fast before she broke her blissfully unaware vow of secrecy.

CHAPTER EIGHT

Lauren Does Her Dinger

I'm like a sixteen-year-old; that's how excited I am at the moment. I'm just about bursting, but I don't want to tell anyone about Oliver yet. It's early days, so I don't want to get ahead of myself, and of course there's Lizzy to think about. I don't want to bring another man into her life and then get her all disappointed if it doesn't work out. Even if I just tell Maureen, she'll tell someone else and then the whole world will know. It's hard to keep your business to yourself in this town, so it's best if I keep my mouth totally shut.

At the end of the Chinese, I was a bit disappointed that Oliver didn't try to kiss me, especially as we had such a good time and we were both a bit tipsy. I'm not talking about anything full on, but a wee kiss on the cheek would have been nice. I thought maybe he wasn't that keen, but then he came into the shop on Saturday morning all smiles and winks, and the next thing I know we're going out again this Friday.

I was having my lunch break at Stone's Café the other day, warming up with some of Maggie's tomato soup, when I saw him walk past. He looked up just as I did, and gave me a wave. He was wearing a dark brown North Face jacket and one of those hats with the earflaps that usually look a bit geeky, but it looked really good on him. I'm sure he'd make anything look good, right enough. When I paid up and left, he was waiting down the road and walked me partway back to the shop. Not all the way, mind. No one saw us together.

"Did you enjoy last Friday night?" he asked.

"I can't remember. I think I drank too much wine."

"Do you want to try again this Friday? We could just go for a walk and avoid alcohol at all costs," he said.

"Sounds good, as long as you buy me a bag of chips."

He said he'd meet me at the end of my road at seven-thirty. I know it must have seemed a bit strange that I didn't want him too near home, but he says he understands that I want to keep a low profile. The girls are going to give me some stick for not going down the social for two weeks in a row, but I don't care. It's ages since I felt excited about anything. A walk and a bag of chips, for God's sake. It's freezing out. But I don't care where we go, or what we do, as long as it's not too public. I just want to get to know him a bit better before I start parading him around the place.

I went over to Maureen's after work today to help her out, like I promised. She seemed shattered; really dead, you know? She answered the door with Kai under her arm and porridge stuck in her hair. I could see bits of it hanging there as if one of the boys had flung the stuff at her. At least she wasn't wearing that awful scarf on her head. I really wanted to tell her about going out this Friday, but I managed to keep it zipped. It was so hard.

"Your timing is perfect, my love," she said. "Kane has discovered how to work Brian's stereo, and Noah has gone purple because he's so hungry."

"Can I take my coat off first?"

"I suppose so, but you don't have time to go to the toilet as well," she said and managed a wee smile.

I chucked my things on the floor in the hallway and made for the kitchen to make a bottle for Noah. He was screaming his head off; he must have been really hungry. I shouted over the noise to Maureen. "Is Brian working late tonight?"

"Aye, of course."

"Do you want me to get you anything for your tea?"

"No, I'll be fine. And Brian will get his tea in the canteen at work. Let's just get these wee ones fed, then I'll be laughing."

I had a sneaky look in the fridge when she wasn't looking and didn't see much in there. I'm worried they're short of money, but I don't know how to ask Maureen about it. She gets really proud and a bit funny if you offer her anything. I offered her some cash once, when I won three hundred pound on the lottery, and she just about bit my head off. "What the hell would I want with your money?" she said. "Away ye go, for goodness' sake." I don't know what to do with her sometimes. I picked Noah up from the floor and stuck a bottle in his mouth. He sucked at it all frantic like he hadn't eaten for a week; it was a shame.

"You and Brian should get out one night, I'll watch the kids for you."

"Thanks, Lauren, but I'm so tired at the moment, I just want my bed."

"Well, just say if you ever want to."

"Brian works late so much anyway, it's not like he wants to go out after," she said. "Although sometimes when he gets into bed, I can smell beer on him."

"Do you think he goes to the pub?"

"Aye, probably."

She turned away and busied herself with the boys. She didn't say anything more, but I could tell it was bothering her. I started to think about it while I was giving the twins a bath, and it all became clear. Brian just doesn't want to come home to the mess and hits the Dalbegie Dram when he isn't doing a late shift. I wonder if the kids go without because of the money he wastes in there. It makes me mad that guys do that, stick their heads in the sand and

Nondescript Rambunctious

pretend like it isn't happening. A few pints and everything gets washed over, the money problems, the kids, the wife struggling back home. Buy a round for your mates and have a laugh like the old days.

When I left Maureen's, I made my way over to the chippy to get me and Lizzy's tea. I felt like I'd been beaten up or something; I was exhausted. I was only over there for a couple of hours; I can't imagine what it's like looking after the boys all day. Granny Mac had it easy with just me and Maureen to deal with. She always said we were real besoms when we were teenagers, but that it was to be expected with girls. I've got it even easier with just my wee angel Lizzy to look after. It's times like this I feel blessed, I really do. If Granny Mac could see her now, she wouldn't believe it.

I have to walk past the pub to get to the chippy, and I stood looking at the big Dalbegie Dram sign hanging outside. I can't remember the last time I was in there; it was probably Maureen's thirtieth a few years ago. I prefer the social. It's less smoky and there's not as many underage drinkers. I'd never really noticed the sign before, but it's old fashioned with a carved blue dog looking at a white duck. The duck has its beak open and looks like it's talking to the dog. It's funny how something can be hanging there for years, but you don't really see it. I looked at my watch; it was seven-thirty. I just had this feeling Brian was going to be in there, drinking his pint and biding his time until the kids were away in bed. And I was right. I was dead on the button. I walked in and there he was, sitting up at the bar having a smoke and a Guinness. I went straight up to him with my hands on my hips, furious I was. I could have belted him.

"I've just been over to your place helping Maureen."

"I've just popped in for a quick pint," he said.

"So that's your first, is it?"

I saw him glance at the barman and widen his eyes, like he was saying keep your mouth shut. "Aye," he said.

"Like hell it is," I said. "You're stinking of booze."

He didn't say anything; just looked into his pint and took a drag of his cigarette.

I went off, did my dinger. "She's really struggling back there. It's not easy bringing up four boys, especially when one's only a baby and your husband's in the pub drinking away half the money. You need to be at home, not in here. She might as well be a single mother the way you carry on. I'm over there helping her out after my day's work, so why can't you do the same, you numpty? What's wrong with you?"

"I'm just having a pint, that's all," he said and took a gulp of his Guinness, flicked his ash on the floor. I heard one of the other guys sniggering.

"You're having a bloody laugh, that's what you're doing. Those boys. They're half yours, you know. And you've an empty fridge at home."

I walked out and I could hear them cheer when the door shut. I imagined them all laughing and slapping Brian on the back. It's okay, pal. They're all the same, the wives, the sister-in-laws, the wee women. Have another pint; don't worry about it. I felt so angry and wanted to go back in there, do another dinger. But I didn't, thank God, I would have made a real fool of myself. I got myself to the chippy and ordered two large fish suppers with pickled onions. There's nothing like it when you've had a long day. The owner of the shop, Jack, wasn't in there, which was a shame because I could have done with a familiar smile and a wee chat right then. A young lad I didn't recognize served up the food while Jack's son Jonno watched from the corner table. Poor wee Jonno is always in there because he doesn't have anywhere else to go and can't be trusted to stay at home on his own, even though he must be twenty-something by now. I'm not sure what's wrong with him, but let's just say he's not quite right. He always gives me a smile, though. He seems happy enough. I waved at him and he went a bit red and grinned down into his lap. He was reading some sort of textbook like the ones you get at school with pictures of molecules or something on the front. I wouldn't put him down for an intellect, but you can't judge.

When I got home, Lizzy was waiting for me in the kitchen with the kettle on.

"I can smell fish suppers!" she shouted as I came in the front door.

"Large ones with pickled onions, you lucky girl," I said.

I put them down on the kitchen table and started to grab some plates and forks from the cupboards. I gave Lizzy a kiss on the cheek, and I swear I could smell whisky or something on her. She had chewing gum in her mouth, probably to disguise it.

"You haven't been drinking, have you?"

"What do you mean?" she said.

"You smell of something."

"No, I don't."

"You'll do yourself some serious damage if you're drinking whisky at your age," I said. "Have you been with that Simon today?"

"I'm not drinking whisky, for God's sake, Mum."

"I'll be watching you, and I'll know if you are. I'm not stupid."

Just when you think things are going right for once, that you've got a nice man on the horizon who's interested in you and not just out for a good time, more worries rise to the surface. Brian in the pub; Lizzy smelling of something I don't want her to smell of. That's two more things to fret about that I don't really need the now. Does it ever end, or do we spend our whole lives worrying about one thing or another? Come to think of it, I don't want to know the answer to that.

CHAPTER NINE

Waiting with Lizzy

Mum didn't come home. She went to the social club like she did every Friday and normally she'd be back by midnight. Half-asleep, I'd always hear her trying to get in the front door, keys jangling as she tried to find the right one. It was comforting in a way, listening as she crept up the stair, stumbled into her bedroom, and threw her shoes on the floor. She got a bit tipsy every week; it was her night out. So what? I didn't care. Sometimes Molly came round and we got a carry-out, a movie, or listened to music or something. It was a laugh. I didn't have anything fancy like Molly did, but my old CD player worked just fine for us when we turned it up loud.

That night was different. I fancied stopping in on my own—watch a bit of telly and read my book in bed. I wanted to write in my diary and just think about stuff. I was still awake reading a magazine at midnight and kept looking at the clock in my room, expecting Mum to come in any minute. At about one o'clock, I was that tired and I fell asleep. Didn't wake up until about eight in the morning. I got up to have a pee and couldn't believe it when she wasn't in her bed.

She'd never left me for a whole night before.

I made myself some toast and tea and watched Saturday

70

morning junk telly for a bit until after nine, when it wasn't too early to phone Molly.

"Mum never came home from the social. Do you reckon it's the boyfriend?"

"Oh my God," Molly said. "That's unbelievable. Has she ever done that before?"

"No, it's not like her to not even phone me. Did you find anything out?"

There was a dramatic pause. "Well. Someone saw her last Friday out with a guy. I asked my mum if she'd heard anything."

"What did you tell your mum for? I thought you were going to be discreet," I said. Molly is that annoying sometimes. She's a gobshite, so she is.

"How else am I supposed to find stuff out? I've got to ask people questions, haven't I? So someone that my mum works with reckons she saw your mum down the Chinese last Friday. She was with some guy, and they were all flirty with each other. Apparently everyone was surprised that she never showed up to the social that night."

"So maybe she never went to the social last night either."

"No, maybe she was out with the guy again and stopped the night with him."

"Oh, crap. That's disgusting, so it is. Well, can you away and find out if she showed up at the social last night?"

"Aye, I'll call you back."

I sat and watched the telly, waiting for the phone to ring again, not really paying attention to what was going on in the program. Mum had work from ten o'clock on Saturday mornings, so I was thinking she'd better come home before then. She wouldn't want to show up to work straight from some guy's house. I didn't want to think about what she might have got up to; you don't want to imagine your own mum doing stuff like that. I looked at the phone, but it didn't ring. It was typical. She wouldn't let me have a mobile, but she had one herself and didn't even know how to use it properly. It probably wasn't even charged up. I went and put the kettle on again in case Mum walked in and needed a tea before work. As I was putting the cups out, the phone finally rang and I jumped on it.

"Molly?"

"Aye, it's me. Your mum never went to the social last night. Sorry, I had to tell my mum that you were worried, and now she's worried about you being on your own. Do you want to come over here?"

"No, I want to be here when she gets home. She's got work at ten."

"We don't know who the guy is. The friend at mum's work couldn't get a good look at him. She said she tried, but they were sitting at the back, right in the corner and it's fair dingy in there."

"It's not that dark in there, is it? I'm surprised she didn't go over there anyway, if she's that nosy."

"Call me later after she's back and gone to work," said Molly. "I want to know who the guy is."

"All right." I put the phone down quick in case Mum was trying to ring.

So she'd been out with some guy all night; that was pure mental. What was she thinking? I wondered if maybe she'd got completely pished and didn't know what she was doing. I was getting a bit angry that she'd left me so I decided to have a bath and get dressed and act like I'd been up all night worrying. That would make her feel bad. I made my bed and filled up the tub with steaming hot water so there wouldn't be any left for her when she got in. It would serve her right. I lay there with it up to my ears, looking at all the tiles on the walls, the bits in between going brown with mould. There were lots of things in our house that were a bit shite.

I couldn't stay in the bath for very long, it was that hot, so I got out and put some clean clothes on. My alarm clock said 9:43. She had to be at work in seventeen minutes. I went downstairs and cleared away my breakfast things, which took a few minutes but still no sign of her. It struck me then that she'd be going straight to work so I got my coat and boots together to go out. I'd march into that shop and tell her thanks very much for calling. It was great that she was so in love but not so good when it made her forget to call her own daughter.

It was cold out, and windy, so I put on Mum's favourite fake-fur hat. She couldn't have a go for borrowing it without asking when she wasn't there to ask. It was dead brilliant; it pulled right down over my ears and kept me warm. I slammed the front door and locked it really careful. I walked slowly down the street, kicking all the leaves as I went, some of them all soggy from the early morning frost. There was no point rushing because she might be late for work anyway. Although not being on time was rare for my mum; she was usually a bit of a fanatic for timekeeping. I had to walk past Molly's to get to the shop, and I ran that bit so they wouldn't see me. I didn't want anyone coming with me; this was between Mum and me.

I walked the long way, down the High Street first, past Dave's Discs and the chippy. When I got to the shop, I stood and looked at it for a minute. What if she wasn't there? It was ten-fifteen by then, so I told myself I was being silly and got myself inside.

"Lizzy! Where the hell is your mum? Don't tell me she's sick."

What a greeting. Jessica was lugging newspapers around for once.

"She's not here then?" I said.

"No, she's not, and I'm doing everything here. I've been in the shop since eight, so the least she could do is be here at ten."

"I don't know where she is, Jessica," I said.

"What do you mean?" She suddenly looked interested, dumped the papers on the floor, and I realized what I was doing. I was almost telling the world's biggest gobshite that my mum didn't come home last night.

I left the shop and ran down the street, swearing out loud. "Shit. Crap. Bloody balls."

Jessica called after me a few times, but I just ignored her. I should have waited a bit longer or just peeked in to see if Mum was there. What an idiot.

Dave's Discs didn't open until eleven, so I wasted some time in Woolies choosing pick-and-mix sweeties and pretending to look at school folders and stuff. Molly once pinched some dead posh pens from there; she put them down the front of her trousers. They lasted us for a whole term at school; it was great. I couldn't do that myself, though. I was way too chicken for stealing. I paid for the sweeties and walked out penless. It was too cold to just wander around the street, so I went into Stone's Café and had a wee pot of tea. They have magazines sitting about in there, and I read and made my tea last as long as I could. Sometimes Mum's friend Maggie worked in there, and I was hoping to talk to her, but she wasn't in that day. There was only one other customer in there, an older guy who kept coughing and wheezing. He was probably a forty-a-day man, the numpty.

It got to nearly half past eleven, and I thought I'd go back to the shop, have a peek through the window, and if she wasn't there, then she obviously wasn't going into work at all. I went the long way around so Jessica wouldn't see me from the tills and had a good look from the side. Mum wasn't there. Jessica was too busy flirting with some guy to notice me, and I just slipped away.

⇒◦⇐

I half-thought Mum might be at home, so I took off her best hat before I opened the front door. The house still smelled of the toast that I'd made in the morning. It was dead quiet and I knew first off that she hadn't been back. There was a message from Molly on the answer phone asking me to give her a call. They all hoped I was all right on my own, which I thought was a bit strange seeing as I was on my own half the time anyway.

I decided to call Auntie Maureen. There was no answer, but I left a message, because you never know. Sometimes she's there but can't get to the phone right away because she's up to her neck in dirty nappies.

"Hello, Auntie Maureen. It's Lizzy. Can you phone me? Mum didn't come home last night and she never showed up at the shop this morning. I thought you might know where she is. Thanks. Bye."

I sat in the silence for a few minutes. The phone didn't ring. I got up again and grabbed my coat, deciding I'd go to Simon's. I knew he'd be in because he doesn't usually get out of bed until late morning at the weekends and has his breakfast at lunchtime. His mum often has a lie even later than that, but that's just her. He lived down towards the river, which is why we started meeting down there and then it just stuck. No one bothered us down there and we didn't bother anyone else. I pulled on the furry hat again and grabbed Mum's best leather gloves, too. Might as well.

Simon was a bit bleary eyed when I got there, even though he'd been up and had some toast already. I was right; his mum was still in bed and he told me she'd been down the social until really late. I told him what was going on and he said he'd wake his mum and ask her if she knew anything. Even though I knew this was a bad idea, I let him. He ran upstairs and left me to shut the front door behind me. Sure enough, I heard her swearing and shouting.

"Jesus fucking Christ, Simon, I was fast asleep. Can you not see that?"

I stared at the floor feeling dead awkward. There were bits of dirt and fluff all over the hallway carpet and leaflets scattered around the doormat, the junk ones you get free. I shuffled them all into a wee pile; I couldn't help myself.

"I need to ask you something. Can you not help me for a minute?"

"Pass me my dressing gown then. I need a pee," she said.

"You know Lizzy's mum, Lauren? Works in the newsagents?"

"Aye, of course I fucking know her. She's the one that thinks she's better than me," she said, "even though I'm not the one who got myself beaten up. At least my men show me some fucking respect."

"Right. Well, did she come to the social last night?"

"I don't think so. Why the hell should I care if she was there or not?"

"You didn't see her?"

"No. Is that it? Can I go for a pish now?"

"You don't know where she was last night?"

"No, I don't. What's wrong with you!"

Simon came downstairs and rolled his eyes. "She didn't see your mum, although she's not really with it," he said.

"Didn't think she would have seen her anyway," I said. "Any more tea going?"

"Aye, let's put the kettle on. I'm not ready to face the world yet."

We sat at the kitchen table, which was covered in crumbs and free newspapers and tea stains. The toilet flushed upstairs and there was some thumping as his mum stumbled back into her room. The door slammed shut. I was dead scared of Simon's mum; she was trouble so she was. I put all the newspapers on the floor and stared at the stains and the bits on the table.

"Are you worried?" he asked.

"I don't know."

"What if she doesn't come home tonight either?"

"I'm not being funny, Simon, but she's not like your mum. She's never done this before. Not left me for a whole night. What if something's happened to her?"

"She's fine," he said. "She'll come back later all hungover and sheepish with two fish suppers. I'm telling you."

"I hope so." I put my head in my hands and tried not to cry. I'd been that angry with her; it hadn't crossed my mind until right then that something might have happened to her. Simon saw my face and came over, rubbed my back. He hugged me from behind, a bit awkward, put his face against mine for a minute. He smelled of sleep and stale cigarette smoke, but I liked it anyway. He could be dead sweet when he wanted to be.

I didn't want to be away from home too long in case Mum showed up or called, so I left Simon's after a wee while and went back. There were two messages, one from Auntie Maureen and another one from Molly. I didn't feel like talking to anyone and sat on the sofa hugging a cushion. I thought about how happy Mum had been recently. And that she hadn't told me that she'd been seeing some guy. Why wouldn't she unless she had something to hide? I just hoped she hadn't got herself into something stupid again. She worried about me and Simon and all that, but she should really have taken a look at herself.

CHAPTER TEN

Oliver's World

My website was called NondescriptRambunctious.com. It didn't provide my main source of income, but it was certainly lucrative.

As well as managing the site, I was a freelance copywriter for many different online companies. Before I went for my spell at HMP Inverness, I had built up a relatively large number of contacts and I had to try to get back in with them again. Fortunately, many of my clients didn't really care who I was, or what my background was, as long as I could deliver what they wanted on deadline. That was the beauty of online work. I wrote search-engine-friendly brand and product descriptions for various marketing companies. I compiled paragraphs for knowledge-based sites about all kinds of things, from retail to food. On occasion, I even created horror stories for the kind of sites that teenagers love to visit behind the backs of their parents. But none of the aforementioned jobs could compete with my very own NondescriptRambunctious.com when it came to life fulfillment. It really was my most creative undertaking.

I had an exclusive audience, a small group who subscribed to my site, and I liked to keep it that way. They were people I happened upon over the years, some from prison, a select few I could trust, who had the same unusual fetishes as me. I couldn't think of a reason why anyone would Google the words Nondescript and Rambunctious together, but if they did, it didn't matter. I had made sure search engines did not index my site. Because it was password-protected, the unwanted web crawlers, the software spiders, couldn't get in and expose its content. And if anyone stumbled across my site by accident—typed in the URL by complete fluke— then they would come across a homepage that looked innocuous and dull. I included far too much type and dark colours so that it was hard on the eye and boring to read. I made it a blog of sorts, by a fictional and socially inept bumbler.

Hi my name is Mr. Rambunctious and I am a budding gardener. I would like to show off my biggest hobby at this time: growing chrysanthemums and other perennial flowering plants.

And so on. I included a photo of an older man that I bought in a secondhand shop for fifty pence. I didn't know who the man was, and didn't think anyone else would either if his picture was being sold as junk. There were other badly shot photos at the bottom of the page, of chrysanthemums and plant pots and the like. It was quite hilarious, and I had great fun making it.

My subscribers knew that if they clicked on the smallest flower on the bottom right-hand side of the screen, the purple one with the long stem, it would take them to the sign-in page. They needed a user name and password to enter the real site—and then an individual, high-security password to get to the core.

This was the part that their subscriptions paid for.

The world is full of evil. There are murderers, rapists, thieves, and pornographers everywhere. It has always been like this. The only difference between the present day and a hundred years ago is the proliferation of the world reporting media. Killing and maiming has become so widespread and exposed that it is a normal part of our society. In any part of the world, in any religion, amongst people of any colour, there are dark things happening. We only need to read a newspaper or watch the news to know this.

What I did went slightly beyond the norm, but really I was just someone going through the motions of everyday abuse. I fed the obsessions of a small group, including myself, of course. We thrived on pain. Not our own pain, but the slow agony of others.

Put in basic terms, we liked to watch people die slowly.

I found that the simplest and cleanest way to kill in slow motion was to starve someone. It was also the least painful way to die in a physical sense, so I was no worse than a murderer who used a knife or blunt instrument. In any case, murder—or "termination" as it is often called—through starvation and dehydration is used worldwide in many medical contexts amongst the elderly, disabled, and brain-damaged. The real pain, the pain that we enjoyed observing, came from the realization, the frustration, and the anger of the victim. So I implemented the capture and everyone else watched the starvation online through real-time video streaming. It was a simple concept, but so effective. To watch a person deflate, psychologically and physically, was truly incredible.

Most of my clients liked to watch a woman on camera, although I didn't perform any sexual acts. My abductions were non-violent and actually quite passive, but still they preferred a female subject. This suited me because I loved the process of capturing a woman. The way I went about it provided me with a challenge, and women liked the initial feeling of being dominated. I enjoyed the thought that a woman had come back to my house because she was attracted to me. She had done it to herself. Once she was through the door, she transformed from a woman to an object, something to study and watch. Everything I had learned about her over the weeks or months of my seduction disappeared, and she converted back to a blank slate.

I had got myself into trouble with the police in the past, but this little secret had never been uncovered. I was extremely careful about where I positioned my camera and my bodies, making sure that even the most thorough search wouldn't find the set-up. My new house in Dalbegie was just perfect. To look at it from the outside, it appeared to be a two-storey cottage, with the main floor at ground level, but in fact it also had my wine cellar underneath, with no windows and only one entrance, through the kitchen pantry floor. The trap door in the corner was just big enough to fit an adult through the opening. There was no handle, just a hole that I could latch my finger into and pull it up. I doubted the previous owner, good old Mrs. Peacock, even knew the cellar was there.

Inevitably, there were no bottles down there, only the remains of some wine racks and old labels on the floor. It was small, so it didn't take long to clean it and wire up the camera and other accessories I needed for the viewing. Afterwards, I laid new wood flooring through the kitchen and pantry for the purpose of hiding the trap door and providing seamless continuity from kitchen to pantry. I created a spring mechanism for the section of flooring covering the trap door, so that it lifted up if you pressed it in the right way. Someone looking in would never know there was anything underneath. So there I had an excellent hideaway for my next NondescriptRambunctious.com project. And Lauren was a perfect subject.

———◦◦◦———

The day after the seduction, I watched the newsagents from my usual spot in the kitchen. Lizzy, the daughter, went looking for Lauren twice. In the morning she went into the shop and came running out again shortly afterwards. Bottle Blond appeared at the doorway and shouted after her, but Lizzy kept on going. It seemed I was not the only one who found Jessica obnoxious.

A man I hadn't seen before, short and red-faced, arrived late morning. I assumed he must be D. McTavish, the owner of the newsagents, whose name is displayed on the shop sign. He didn't look very happy and did not come back out again for some hours.

I thought it strange how he had so little hands-on dealings with the place and wondered if it would do him good to spend time in the store for a change, instead of leaving two women to run his business for him. Not something that I would have done.

I grabbed my hat and coat and went to get my daily newspaper, perversely interested to see how Jessica would act in the presence of D. McTavish. To my disgust, she behaved just as badly, if not worse than usual. The minute I set foot in the door, she was on top of me, breathing down my neck, her rancid perfume making me feel nauseated.

"Here's one of our regulars," she said. "Come in for the *Times*, have you?"

"You are correct, well done," I said and walked pointedly to the till, where D. McTavish was sorting through money with a face of stone.

"Lauren's let us down today," she called out.

"Oh?" I held out my money.

"Didn't turn up and hasn't even called," she said. "Her wee daughter was in here earlier looking for her, the poor lamb. Derek's not too happy about it, are you, Derek?"

Derek grunted and handed me some change. I began to realize why he kept away from his business. He obviously took no pleasure in dealing with people.

"I expect she has good reason," I said as I left the shop.

"She better have," said Jessica.

If she knew, perhaps she would have kept that brazen red mouth of hers shut.

⟨━◆━⟩

Lizzy reappeared later and looked through the window at the side of the shop. When she left, she seemed despondent and vulnerable and I was tempted to go after her, but I told myself to calm down

Nondescript Rambunctious

and take one thing at a time. I had a tendency to want to start new projects before the old ones were completed and had to stop myself with a firm hand. Concentrate on the now. In any case, to have two abductions in such a short space of time would have created far more suspicion. As it was, no one could guess what had happened to Lauren. Had she been abducted, or had she gone missing? Had she had an accident and lost her memory? Left the country because she couldn't cope any more? There's always an element of doubt with a disappearance. But two people gone; now that's a potential pattern of abduction.

I had a brand-new notebook and ballpoint pen ready to take notes on Lauren. How she collapsed, gave up, how long it took, any particular findings that I hadn't noticed with previous projects. Fresh white pages ready for a fresh observation; there was nothing more satisfying. All statistics and details were for my own enjoyment, and I didn't post them on my website. Not everyone wanted to know the minutiae that I found so fascinating. I hid the notebook underneath another section of my new floorboards because it would have provided a tragic piece of evidence should anyone have found it. I had seventeen notebooks in all and kept them in a safety deposit box. Seventeen observations in ten years. I tried to stick with one body per year as I found that keeping numbers down worked both to keep my subscribers' anticipation levels raised and to keep suspicion to a minimum. But sometimes things happened to increase the numbers.

I think the first project I worked on, back in 1997, was the most interesting. Perhaps it was because it was my first time and everything was relatively new, but then again I definitely did not see anything like it with anyone else. Her name was Cassandra; she was thirty-three years old and in incredible shape. I had almost forgotten that I was going through the motions of capture when I got her back to my apartment and was momentarily tempted to have a night of debauchery in the form that she obviously wanted.

But the moment passed, of course.

I was living in Dunblane at the time, and we had walked up two steep hills to get home. I remember marvelling that she wasn't anywhere near out of breath. Of course when she regained consciousness and discovered that she was strapped down and linked up to the online experience, she battled and fought like a tiger, fully aware of her surroundings. Lack of nourishment slowed her down after twenty-four hours, but she kept fighting quite strongly for five days. Then on the sixth day, just before slipping into a coma, she seemed to go into a complete state of euphoria. She shut her eyes, relaxed, and made little moaning noises for some hours. It was as if she was having the deepest, most intense kind of pleasure. It was extremely erotic to watch and my subscribers loved it. We thrived on people's pain, but that little window of ecstasy amidst the agony was a joy to watch. With each victim I managed to seduce, I yearned that it might happen again. I hoped that Lauren might deliver; something about her felt just right.

CHAPTER ELEVEN

Lauren in the Bright Lights

Granny Mac? I can talk to you in my head, can't I? I think you can hear me up there; we were always in tune. I hope you can't see this, though. I can see myself. I'm looking down on my naked body; it's like I'm dead or nearly dead. I might be in a dream. I'm not sure.

Here I am, lying on a hard table in the dark. There's a video camera on one side, always running. The whir of the mechanics is the only sound in the place. I'm so scared but I can't feel my heart beating or my pulse quickening; I'm numb. I should be cold; I can see goosebumps on my skin, but I can't feel anything either.

Oliver. I was out with him; that's the last thing I can remember. We went back to his place, and he appeared from the kitchen with a bottle of posh stuff; can't remember what it was called. Beautiful crystal glasses, him so gentlemanly. Pouring a drink for me carefully so it didn't spill.

"Let's toast to us," he said.

"To us." I took a big sip and felt the bubbles all warm down my throat.

I'm strapped down at my ankles and neck with thin, yellow rope. I can see it digging in. I'm not straining against it, but it's still making red marks on my skin. So tight. There's another sound, a faint one. It could be my own blood pumping through my veins.

Even in the dead of night, or in the early hours of the morning, whichever way you look at it, I can normally hear things from my bedroom. A distant lorry starting up, the wind rustling in the trees, maybe an early bird calling out for morning. But here there's nothing but the whir and that faint throb of blood. Either I'm in the quietest place in Scotland or I'm underground.

We walked along the river in the moonlight. The chip supper was my idea. It was a stupid idea. I thought we'd be sharing chips and walking under the full moon, holding hands. It would be cold and we'd cuddle up together. In reality, he didn't touch me at all and I felt disappointed again, let down. Then he asked me back to his. I was that taken aback, I just said yes off the bat. Before he changed his mind. I just wanted to spend some more time with him and get out of the freezing wind that I hadn't thought about when I planned this stupid intimate evening. I wasn't expecting anything big would happen; I just wanted to talk, find out more about him. The next thing I remember is the fizz, those tall glasses. Me wondering if he'd planned to ask me back all along. He was standing in front of me with a look on his face, a sort of longing look that made me feel dead special. Where had I seen that expression before? I think you know, Granny Mac. And so do I now.

We sat down on his sofa; it was quite modern and bright red. The material felt smooth, cool. I thought to myself, How did he not have any photos about the place?

Then nothing. Blackness.

The dark and the silence drag on.

I'm falling somewhere. Everything so heavy.

CHAPTER TWELVE

Sinking in for Lizzy

I stopped being angry with Mum for not coming back. She was properly gone, and I was worried and sick and terrified. But not cross anymore. That first day I didn't answer the phone at home because I didn't really know what to say to anyone. I even wished I hadn't left that message for Auntie Maureen, don't know what I was thinking. Eventually, she came knocking at the door. I knew she would, that I'd have to speak to her. She started asking me loads of questions. It was brutal.

"What does she think she's playing at?"

"Who was she with last night?"

"Where did they go if they didn't go to the social?"

"Why did she not say anything to me the other day?"

"When will she be back?"

It went on and on, and I kept shrugging my shoulders and saying "I don't know" until she stopped asking. Wee Noah was grizzling because he was teething, and that was making it more stressful. Auntie Maureen kept sticking her finger in his mouth and rubbing his gums, which made him cry even more. In the end, she insisted that I go and stay at her and Uncle Brian's until Mum showed up again. I told her I was all right on my own, but she wouldn't have any of it. I liked going over there sometimes; my cousins are dead cute so they are, but I'm always glad to leave again. They're so noisy and never give it a rest. But I had to go with it, me being only twelve and all.

I packed a rucksack with two sets of clothes and my shampoo and stuff, thinking that would be more than enough because I'd probably be back the next day. But I wasn't. All weekend I slept in wee Noah's room, on a blow-up bed next to his crib. He went in with Auntie Maureen and Uncle Brian. Uncle Brian didn't seem too happy about it because he liked his sleep and Noah woke up sometimes at night crying, but he didn't say anything. Noah had stick-on stars on his ceiling that glowed in the dark. When the lights were all off at night, I felt like I was camping outside. It was actually quite good, like I was floating. It also gave me something to look at while I wasn't sleeping for wondering where my mum was.

The last time I'd stayed over at Auntie Maureen's was after that last beating that Mum got from Dad. She had to go to hospital for a couple of days in the end. They thought I wouldn't really know what was going on, but I did. I could hear Auntie Maureen on the phone going off about it to her friends for a start. Being there again brought back a lot of memories about that time, all the fights and the crying. I was glad when it all ended, when Dad went away, leaving me and Mum to ourselves. But now I was so scared that she was beaten up again somewhere, not wanting me or anyone else to see her face. I wouldn't care how bad she looked; I just wanted her back with me.

———✦———

Auntie Maureen had said right away that we should call the police and report my mum missing. She said it wasn't like her to just go off like that and we shouldn't assume anything. Uncle Brian agreed, but then again he went along with most things she said. I didn't normally see Uncle Brian very much because he worked all the time, so it was funny staying there and watching him and Auntie Maureen together. She was quite bossy to him really, although she wasn't as tough as my mum. Mum said that younger sisters were a total pain in the arse until you both got into your thirties and then they became just a bit of a pain in the arse. She didn't really mean it, but I saw Auntie Maureen did seem to get her own way most of the time.

When she rang the police on Saturday, she told me to leave the room so it didn't upset me, but I listened from the stair. It wasn't difficult to hear her, because she had to shout over the chimp noises that wee Noah was making. I never said anything, but he looked a bit like a chimp as well because his ears stuck out like Uncle Brian's and he had a lot of thick, black hair. She put on a different voice like she was a receptionist in a posh hotel or something.

"My sister went missing last Friday night and we're very worried about her. She has a twelve-year-old daughter, my niece, whom we've got staying with us. No, it's not like her to disappear like that. No, she hasn't done it before; we can't quite believe it. She went out and never came back. We don't know where she went. No, we don't know that either. No. What! Three days? But she's missing the now; we know that the now. Tuesday morning? You're joking aren't you?"

By the end, she forgot the posh voice. Apparently, you could only be missing if you'd been away three days. So we had to wait and officially report Mum missing on Tuesday. To me, that seemed like forever. There I was on Saturday night under Noah's glo-stars in my jammies wondering whether it would ever come. Surely she'd show up by then anyway?

Auntie Maureen did a roast beef dinner on Sunday, made a big fuss and even made her own gravy. Uncle Brian ate like he hadn't had a proper meal for weeks. I wasn't hungry and so he even had my Yorkshire pudding. The kids dropped most of theirs on the floor and there was a lot of washing up to do after, but it passed the time until I could go back to bed again.

⤜⬥⤛

Monday was the hardest day. There was still no word from anyone and Auntie Maureen called the rest of Mum's friends. I had to get out of the house and see Simon, made some excuse about getting some fresh air. She waved me off, probably wanting to spout off on the phone while I wasn't there. I couldn't go and see Molly on the way because she'd be at school. Auntie Maureen said I didn't have to go in if I didn't want to, so I gave it a miss. No doubt Simon was skiving off as well. Sometimes his mum made him stay home so he could look after her, make her cups of tea and nurse her latest hangover, so she signed sick notes and everything. I didn't know if I was jealous of that or not; it just seemed wrong.

I ran all the way to Simon's house, dead excited to see him because we hadn't hung out since the Friday. I went the long way because I didn't feel like going along the river by myself, I don't know why. It didn't feel safe now. The upstairs curtains were all drawn so his mum was still in her bed. I knocked the door quietly and looked through the letter box. I whispered through it. "Simon? It's me, Lizzy. Are you there?"

I heard something drop on the floor in the front room, some shuffling about.

"Simon? Is that you?"

I was trying to whisper loudly but not too loud in case I woke his ratty mum up. There was a murmur of voices and then he appeared in the hallway, saw me looking. He didn't say anything, just flapped his hand as if he was shooing away a fly.

"What's going on?"

"Go away," he said quietly. "I'll see you later."

"When?"

He didn't answer, just held up his hand and shook his head. Then he turned away and went back into the front room. I heard some more low voices. I couldn't believe it. He even knew about my mum. What was he doing? Who was so important in that room he couldn't even talk to me for a minute? It was a man's voice, not some other girl, but I still felt dead rejected, really down about things then. I walked slowly back home with my hands in my pockets, looking at the floor so I didn't catch anyone's eye that might know me. I didn't feel like talking to anyone and played the game where you can't step on any cracks in the pavement or sticks in the gutter, just to keep my mind on something.

My life was just getting worse.

I went home instead, to get more clothes. Auntie Maureen had even more washing to do with me around. I'd never seen so much washing in my life; there were piles of it everywhere, and that was just for the boys. Uncle Brian seemed to wear the same thing every day, and I reckoned it was because he felt guilty putting anything in the wash. I'm not kidding, he had a navy blue shirt on his back for days; it was stinking.

I had a daydream on the way back home that Mum was in the kitchen, with the kettle on, in a huff with me for not being there when she got back. I'd say, Well, what do you expect, leaving me on my own for days on end. And she'd give me a hug and tell me she was sorry and get fish suppers. But the house was empty, and smelled of dust and stale bread. I collected all the post and put it on the kitchen table, watered Mum's yucca plant in the hall, and threw out the carton of milk that was going off in the fridge. I did those jobs all the time, so it was nothing, but it felt weird for some reason. Like it was final. I wanted to stay, sit on the sofa in the peace and quiet and watch telly for a bit, but Auntie Maureen said I had to go straight back to hers. I just sat there for a wee minute and listened to the house. Mum's alarm clock was making a funny noise like the battery was running out; I could hear it faintly up the stair. If I closed my eyes and concentrated really hard, I could smell her coming in the room, dressed up for Friday night. A bit of that posh perfume that she only wore when she went out because she said it was a waste in the day. I wouldn't think it was a waste if she wore it all the time. It was her smell, wasn't it?

⇒≻◆≺

Tuesday finally came. Auntie Maureen called the police back, and I listened to that conversation from the stair as well, this time with Kai and Kane wrapped around my neck. They were playing peek-a-boo with each other using my head as a shield.

"She's still missing, just like I said. No, we still don't know who she was with or where she went. Yes, that's three days. Her daughter? Yes, she's still here and she can stay for as long as it takes. Right. See you later then."

Auntie Maureen called me downstairs and I picked up the twins, one under each arm, which they found really funny. They were heavy as anything, so they were.

"The police are coming round in a bit. Finally. They'll ask us a load of questions, so we need to have a good old think about what we know and if we can remember anything that might be important."

I had been thinking of something that might be possible but had been keeping it to myself. In any case, Auntie Maureen had been so busy ringing around Mum's friends and the few other drabs of family all weekend that she didn't have time to listen to what I had to say. Nobody seemed to know where exactly Mum went on Friday night or who she was with. The only person that knew anything at all was that woman at Molly's mum's work. The one that thought she saw my mum with some guy in the Chinese. But she didn't get a good look at the guy, so it was kind of useless. At least we knew there was someone Mum was hiding, and that she might be with him. That was the part that I'd been thinking about. There was definitely someone she might want to keep secret— my dad. If she was back with him, now that wouldn't exactly be something she'd broadcast.

"Auntie Maureen? Have you phoned my dad?"

"Oh God, no. I haven't." She looked at me, hands on her hips, and I looked back at her and shrugged.

"You don't think. I mean, she wasn't. Or did you just mean," she struggled.

Auntie Maureen was getting all in a tizzy, and I just shrugged again. How the hell was I supposed to know if she was back with my dad? I was just their only daughter; it's wasn't that I mattered or anything. I told her his number was in Mum's address book back home.

"He lives in Yorkshire now and that's why I only see him once a year," I said.

"I know that, darling, but I tell you what," she said. "You go on and get the book. Then we'll have it here when the police come over. It might be better if they call him because I don't know what to say to that man, I really don't. If she's with him, then I'll skelp her, so I will, and I'll kill him."

"Right then, I'll go now," I said.

I was glad to get away because Noah had started to cry again and Kai and Kane were pushing all the buttons on the television, which was really annoying. I'd been spending a lot of time looking after those two imps while Auntie Maureen had been busy on the phone. Sometimes it seemed as if she was enjoying it, like it was giving her a break from other things. Getting them dressed in the morning and playing with them for an hour was exhausting, so it was. Even Billy was hard work, though he was supposed to be the big brother. Boys are rubbish, so they are.

"Be back within the hour, Lizzy, don't forget the police are coming."

I grabbed my coat and Mum's furry hat and ran out before Auntie Maureen gave me any messages to get. I just wanted to be at home for a bit, alone. When I got there, it looked dull from the outside. The brightness had gone out of the green door, and the plants on the front porch were withered. I hadn't noticed these things the day before. The days were getting darker, and things were starting to look different because of it. Or maybe it was just because I had a funny feeling in my stomach and nothing seemed right. I chose that green paint with Mum. We both loved it, agreed straight away that was the colour we'd get. It was dead cool, the brightest colour in the shop. It had faded now.

I sat on the doorstep for a bit, picked at the fuzz on the doormat. I didn't fancy hanging about inside, so I ran in and grabbed the address book from the hall and left before I had a chance to feel how empty the place was again. Then I ran back to Auntie Maureen's, not even looking over at Molly's in case her mum was there to stop me and ask more questions. I arrived just as a police car pulled up. Two of them got out, a man and a woman, both putting their hats on as they stood up. Then it hit me that this could be serious. Something really bad could have happened to Mum. My heart thumping, I felt sick as I walked up to the door. I tried my hardest not to cry although I really wanted to.

"Lizzy Finning?"

I nodded and looked up at the sky, so my tears wouldn't fall out.

"Let's go inside, shall we?"

CHAPTER THIRTEEN

Oliver's Interview

Notes—Experiment Number Eighteen
Start Date: Saturday 17 November
End Date: (tbd)
Place: Dalbegie, Scotland
Age of Body: 41
Est. Weight of Body: 155 lb
Name of Body: Lauren

Day 1, Sat 17 Nov: My concoction of champagne with Rohypnol last night may have been too strong as body number eighteen (Lauren) has been in a state of unconsciousness for longer than usual. No spotlights or camera today, as there's little to see; however, will begin the showing tomorrow. Linked up catheters and secured all bindings whilst she slept. Not much sign of movement as yet, although there is some evidence of straining at the ankles.

⬥

There was a subtle change of atmosphere. I noticed a new, bitter edge to the wind. The leaves almost finished dropping and the colours of autumn were either sodden on the ground or swept away, not flitting in the air like they had been in recent weeks. The pensioners arriving at the shop mid-morning wore hats and gloves to keep out the cold. I saw many ugly pairs of those camel-coloured zipped fur boots.

As I was watching, two policemen arrived on foot and went inside the newsagents for a good half an hour. I assumed they were interviewing D. McTavish and Bottle Blond, and good luck to them if they thought they would get two words out of him or a modicum of sense out of her. The mute and one of the most irritating women I had ever met.

Women. On the one hand, they're all about feminist values and camaraderie, but really they can't stand each other. Women are always badmouthing their own sex and envious when one of their peers is more successful than them. Men frustrate them and women exasperate them; you can never please a woman. When I was in my twenties and more fresh faced and naive, I did stumble across Helen, who was quite different from any other woman I'd met or have met since. She taught me a few things in life, particularly when we discovered we were on similar paths in life.

⟫━◆━⟪

Day 2, Sun 18 Nov: Switched on spotlights and camera for twenty-four hour observation. The cellar is becoming hotter in the lights than previous venues, due to lack of ventilation. This may have repercussions on decay of the body. Lauren woke up, blinking rapidly under the lights. Apparent confusion as to whereabouts; however, little dialogue is forthcoming at this stage. Minor lacerations of wrists, ankles, and neck where she has worked against the bindings.

⟫━◆━⟪

When I met Helen, I thought she was fascinating from the beginning. We were both working a community service period at the Cat Rescue Society in Edinburgh. She was already ensconced in the program when I arrived, and they assigned her to show me what to do. The community service essentially involved cleaning out litter trays and making sure the kittens didn't make too much of a mess of their living areas. We were encouraged to play with the animals, but Helen and I didn't bother too much with that and just got on with the job. We bonded instantly, which took me by surprise because I am not usually eager to make acquaintances with women that I don't find physically attractive. Her short bowl cut was very unflattering to her round face, and I couldn't tell where her waist was. She was, however, extremely sharp, and had a dry, resigned attitude that I liked. She didn't particularly enjoy the work, yet she focused intently on each of her tasks so that they were carried out as meticulously as I would do myself.

"I won't ask what you did to deserve community service," she said as we carried out buckets of soapy water to the cat cages.

"And I won't ask you either," I said.

"It's because I couldn't really give a shit what you did," she said. "It's not that I'm being polite."

"Well, I was being polite, so I suppose that makes me a better person."

That's how the conversation went most of the time. Short and sharp. She opened one of the wire cages and stepped inside, motioned for me to follow. There were sixteen cats inside and five litter trays, all smelling rancid. She picked one up, emptied the contents into a bin bag and threw it down again, making one of the cats jump. Then she took out a hard-bristled brush from one of the buckets and started to scrub the tray ferociously.

"Just grab one of the other trays and get going," she said. "It's not pretty, but it's got to be done."

I had brought my own industrial-strength rubber gloves and

was glad of them. I pulled them out of my coat and put them on, much to her amusement.

"Don't ruin your nails, will you."

We had thirty days working together at the Cat Rescue, which was a long time to spend with anyone, let alone a hobbit of a woman with attitude, and fortunately after a few days we started to bond. My obsessive hygiene, combined with her meticulousness, made us a good cleaning team, and we usually managed to finish our tasks well before the end of the day. Sometimes we had a whole hour to sit and talk behind one of the cat cages, our hands throbbing from scrubbing and wiping.

If someone asked me what we talked about at first, I really wouldn't be able to say. Life in general, what we'd done, where we'd been. But somehow we found that we had a common interest and that is what led to our partnership, albeit a brief one. Of course, this was before the birth of NondescriptRambunctious.com, but what we did together helped to shape things to come in my life. She eventually became one of my most trusted subscribers and a champion of my site. There are not many women for whom I have a healthy respect without any kind of desire. Indeed, there is only the one.

⤐⬥⟵

Day 3, Mon 19 Nov: Received three messages today, including one from Helen, regarding the excellent calibre of Lauren. Her naked torso looks good considering age and weight. She is fully conscious and awake; deeper lacerations have occurred in areas of bindings, showing further resistance. There has been some dialogue regarding the usual questions of how and why, plus empty threats of revenge and complaints of thirst. Her conscious mind is in full working order. Her throat is becoming dry, her voice cracked. Hair is very greasy; body odour is minimal. Dark amber urine observed through catheter in small amounts. The first three days have shown the usual symptoms of realization, early dehydration, and panic.

⬗◆⬖

Mahatma Gandhi, in his campaign for India's independence, survived for twenty-one days without food. He did, however, allow himself small amounts of water. Hunger strikes can go on for much longer than that, but again in these cases the campaigners or protesters allow themselves to drink. Near starvation like this can continue, without fatality, for a lot longer than total starvation. There was even a medical experiment in the seventies where they put obese people on a starvation diet for forty days and they all survived. Again, they were allowed water.

I liked to completely starve my subjects, which meant definitely nothing to drink. The consequences were more noticeable, more immediate. The death remained slow in relative terms, but there were more marked changes to observe. The longest any of my subjects survived was nine days without food or water; it was during experiment number eight, when the body was overweight, yet at twenty-one was relatively young and healthy. I predicted body number eighteen wouldn't last the week, being no spring chicken.

Late in the afternoon there was a knock at the door while I was just coming up the stairs of the cellar. Fortunately, Lauren had drifted into sleep and wasn't making any noise as I opened the trap door and stepped out into the pantry. I very much doubted that anything could be heard from outside the house in any case. I carefully replaced the fake wood floor and peered out of the kitchen window before answering. It was the same two police officers that had been at the newsagents, one female and one male. I removed my rubber gloves and put them in the kitchen sink before answering.

"Good afternoon, officers."

"Good afternoon, sir," said the woman. "PC Jane Smyth and PC Michael Donaldson. Can we have a quick word?"

They couldn't have been taking the disappearance very seriously if they only had a couple of PCs on the job. PC Michael Donaldson looked like he was only just old enough to drink.

"Of course," I said. "Won't you come in? What is this about?"

They didn't answer. I took them into the conservatory at the back of the house where I'd put a secondhand sofa, two wooden chairs, and a small table. I had bought a silver picture frame from a charity shop and inserted the only photograph I owned in an attempt to make the room homely. It was of my father, in full naval uniform, standing on the dock at Portsmouth. He wasn't smiling. I motioned them to sit down on the sofa and perched myself on one of the chairs. Although the cellar was soundproofed, I didn't want to take any chances and felt secure in the knowledge that my conservatory was at the opposite end of the house.

"I'm Oliver Jenkins, by the way. How can I help you?"

PC Jane Smyth took off her hat and smoothed down a mousey brown ponytail. Her hair was too long, something that made me cringe. It also looked a little unwashed, greasy at the scalp. She saw me watching her and blushed a little. PC Michael Donaldson took out a notebook and studied me intently.

"We're asking people in the neighbourhood if they know of the whereabouts of Lauren Finning. She works in the newsagents just over the road so you must know her."

"Yes, I know her. I didn't know her surname, but there can only be one Lauren that works in the newsagents over the road." I smiled.

He smiled back. "She went out on Friday night and didn't come home. Her daughter hasn't seen or heard from her since. Do you know anything about who she was with, or where she could have gone?"

"No. I really don't know her that well; I haven't lived here very long. She just sells me my newspaper every day."

"The *Times*," said PC Jane Smyth.

"That's right," I said.

"Do you know what she usually does of a Friday night?"

"I have no idea," I said. "The girl that she works with often tries to talk me into going to the Dalbegie Dram. Perhaps she went there?"

"No, she didn't," said PC Michael Donaldson.

"Have you ever been to the pub with her?" asked PC Jane Smyth.

"No. Like I said, I don't know her. I'm not really a pub person either. I keep to myself."

"What do you do of a Friday night, Mr. Jenkins?"

"I stay at home. I'm a quiet person and I don't have friends here yet."

"So you don't know anyone around here that well?"

"No, so I'm afraid I can't be of much help to you."

I smiled again and they looked at me a little blankly. PC Michael Donaldson put away his notebook and they stood up to leave. I looked at each of them directly and said that I hoped Lauren would turn up soon. I knew that as long as I looked them in the eye, they would believe that I was being sincere. It was such a simple rule, but so effective. PC Jane Smyth even flashed me a smile as she left, the stupid little greasy police whore.

CHAPTER FOURTEEN

Lizzy Alone

The police knew eff-all. They were as useless as they were on the telly. It was already Wednesday, the fifth day that Mum had been gone, if you didn't include the Friday night. That was too long, so it was, and I was in a right mess. Molly had been finding out a few bits of information, but I didn't know which parts were made up by folk and which parts were true. Her mum knew pretty much everyone in town, and there was a lot of talk about what had happened. I had a feeling that I wasn't being told some of the theories. I was sure Jessica in the shop would tell me if I asked her, but I wasn't ready to face her yet.

Auntie Maureen said I could have the rest of the week off school if I wanted to, said she'd write me a note saying I was stressed. So I had the week off. Of course I did. Normally I'd be dead chuffed, but I didn't exactly feel like celebrating. I spent a lot of time in wee Noah's room that had suddenly become "my room," crying. I couldn't help it; the tears just came and then all of a sudden I'd be greetin' like a baby. I was dead worried about everything. It wasn't right, disappearing like that for such a long time. If she'd done a dirty, just the one night, I'd have understood. I'd have been a bit cross and milked it for a while, but what's the one night? If it was the weekend and she'd been down to see my dad or something, it would have been odd that she didn't tell me. She might have been really stressed out and embarrassed about it, and I would have understood eventually. But five days? There was something very wrong. That wasn't her.

When I thought about her, really imagined her face, I got a pain in my chest and couldn't breathe. I just couldn't believe it was happening to me.

The trouble with not going to school was that I didn't get to see Molly much. Auntie Maureen let me go over to hers one day before tea, but it was only for an hour. Molly was dead nice, gave me a hug, and made me a hot cocoa with a chocolate finger to dip in. We had a good chat about everything, but I'm not sure if it made me feel better or not. I gave her a note to give to Simon for me, if she saw him at school. Even if he wanted to explain what it was all about that day at his house, he couldn't because he didn't even know where Auntie Maureen stayed. I put down the address and phone number, said I needed to see him, and signed it "Lizzy" with no "love" or kisses or anything. I didn't want him to think it was some cheesy love letter. Molly put the note in her bag. I knew she'd read it, so that was the other reason I kept it short. I trusted that she'd give it to him though, because it would make her feel important, like she was in the know or something like that.

We talked about my dad. After a while, Molly started slagging him and what he used to do, but I didn't need her to remind me. Aye, he was a pig all right. I should know because I lived with him for the first ten years of my life. She told me that a lot of people had been saying my dad was back and he'd beaten Mum up so she wouldn't come home. She didn't want me or anyone else to see her swollen face. Three people thought they'd seen him around the town. But nobody was sure. There were no facts.

"So apparently the guy your mum was with the other week, the one in the Chinese, he could easily have been your dad. He was tall with brown hair. That woman at Mum's work said she's remembering more things about him. Do you think they were seeing each other again?"

"My dad lives in Yorkshire."

"I know, but he could have come up to see her, stayed with someone."

"Who? The police have been down to his place; they've talked to him. She wasn't down there and he hadn't come up here."

"So he says."

"Molly, I don't think it was him, seriously. My mum's not that stupid to be back with him, after he kicked her about. He's my dad and everything, but he's not exactly God's gift is he. The police have interviewed people that he said he was with on Friday night. He was in Yorkshire, without my mum. I reckon that's no lie," I said.

She looked at me and frowned. "I'm still a bit suspicious."

So was I a bit suspicious, but I didn't let on. I was pretty sure the police would be able to tell if Dad was lying. And if they were down in Yorkshire together, why the hell wouldn't Mum phone? It didn't make any sense. If she was beat up, she'd still call me. Wouldn't she?

"They're going to check Mum's bank records. Then they'll know if she's been spending money somewhere else, like Yorkshire," I said.

"It's like something off the telly, so it is." Molly went off on a bit of a daydream. She'd got a crush on some guy in *The Bill*.

"Well, it's real and it's happening to me."

Molly looked sorry then and snapped out of the wee time she was having to herself. "I'm sorry, Lizzy. I am, honest. She'll be back soon."

"I know." I dumped myself on one of their comfy armchairs and hugged a cushion. No one was sure of anything. There was so much crap flying around. I didn't know she'd be back soon; how could I? The only thing I could do was hope.

━━◆◆━━

That night, Auntie Maureen's phone rang, and she threw wee Noah at me and went to answer it. It was like she got a kick out of gabbing about what was happening, couldn't wait to grab that phone to see who was on the other end. She really annoyed me sometimes. Anyway, her face fell a mile and she held the phone away from her face like it was contaminated or something.

"It's your dad."

I gave her back Noah, who wriggled and screeched then let off a big one. I took the phone, clearing my throat like it was someone important to speak to. I have to say, I felt really nervous, which is silly because he was only my dad. Auntie Maureen mouthed the words, "Be careful what you say," which made me more nervous.

"Hi, Dad. You got my message, then."

"Hello, my wee darling. Are you okay? Sorry I've taken so long to call back."

I relaxed, turned to look out the window. "Aye, I'm okay. Do you know where Mum is?"

"She's not showed up yet, then? I had the police down here asking all sorts. I says, as if she'd be down here with me. I'm the last person she'd want to be with."

"That's what I thought," I said.

He laughed loudly, and muttered some more stuff about how daft it was to think she'd be with him. "And you're all right staying at your Auntie Maureen's, then?"

"What if I wasn't?"

"Are you not?"

I was tempted to say I wasn't all right just to see what he'd do, but I didn't really want to know. Knowing him, he'd just leave me there anyway, even if I was about to top myself.

"Aye, I'm okay," I said.

"Do you have any idea where your mum might be?"

"I really don't know, Dad. She's just disappeared into thin air, so she has. What if she doesn't come back?"

"She'll be back, hen. Don't worry yourself. Was she seeing anyone? Any men about the place?"

"No. Will I see you at Christmas, Dad?"

"Of course you will, my darling. Have a think about what you want for a present. I'll get you anything you want, okay?"

It didn't seem quite right talking about Christmas already, but that was the only time I saw my dad, and I couldn't think of anything else to say to him. He said I'd got to call him as soon as I heard anything about Mum, but I wasn't sure why he suddenly cared what happened to her. Unless he was just worried that he might get stuck with me if she didn't come back. He'd shacked up with some woman called Sharon, who was much younger than Mum and a legal secretary. I wasn't sure what that was, but it sounded dead posh. I hadn't met her, but I could just imagine what she was like because he always told me wee things about her when I saw him, even though I didn't really want to know. She was blond with long legs and had a really quiet voice. And she was clever as well as dead pretty, or so he said. She sounded a bit too perfect. I never told Mum because she might have got upset. No, he wouldn't want me down in Yorkshire. I'd just get in the way of him and his new clever, pretty, blond punch bag.

When I was off the phone, Auntie Maureen quizzed me. She wanted to know exactly what he'd said, word for word. She tutted at everything, even when I told her he'd said, "Don't worry yourself." I thought maybe he just called to see if I was okay, but Auntie Maureen reckoned there was something more to it, something sinister. She gave wee Noah back to me with a bottle of milk and a bib, said she had to go see to the twins and give them their dinner. I'd fed the baby loads of times by then. I sat on the sofa with the telly on, him on my lap, leaning back on my chest so I could smell his wee head and nuzzle into his hair. He had wispy hair; it was dead soft. We watched a repeat of *Friends*, the one where Chandler looks too thin and Monica shags him. Noah went all floppy and sat there with a bottle in his mouth. He was so cute.

Nondescript Rambunctious

I always wished I could have had a brother, and once asked Mum why there was only me. She went a bit red and said that by the time she decided on another baby, she and my dad split. But I could tell there was something else she wasn't telling me. I never asked her again, though. Some things are best left, Molly said.

The next morning Uncle Brian left the house at six o'clock; I heard the front door slam. I looked out of the window and saw him walking fast up the road, his coat collar turned up and his hat pulled over his ears. He was hunched over in the cold. I felt sorry for him sometimes. He always looked like he could do with a good sleep and a shot of whisky. I pretended to sleep in until ten because I couldn't face going downstairs and answering Auntie Maureen's questions with the boys shouting around us. I kept hearing wee Noah crying, but I put my pillow over my head and it drowned it out a bit. Every time I shut my eyes, Mum appeared in front of me, all smiles like she was when she'd just bought my birthday present and wanted to tell me what it was. It was like torture, and in the end I got up because even Noah's crying and the twins' screeching was better than that.

I spent most of the day helping Auntie Maureen and mooching around the house. Then in the afternoon, a letter got put through the door. Auntie Maureen pounced on it and then looked through the letter box to see who had put it through, but she didn't see anyone, thank God.

"It's for you," she said after turning it over a few times and holding it up to the light. She watched while I started to open it, so I ran up the stair to my room to read it. How rude is that, but I didn't care because I recognized Simon's writing on the envelope.

She shouted after me, "Who's it from, hen?"

"Molly."

"Why's Molly sending you a letter? Did you not see her yesterday?"

"Aye." I shut my bedroom door and opened the letter carefully so that the envelope didn't tear and I could keep it just the way it came. It wasn't very long, and you could really tell that Simon missed a lot of school.

> *Lizzy,*
> *Mums got a new boyfrend his name is Roy and he is a dealer and a right basterd. He is making me work fer him and Im not to see my frends. See you when I can.*
> *Simon.*

His mum had been hanging out with losers for years, but this one sounded like he would win the top prize for being the biggest ned. Right when I needed Simon, he had to get involved with Roy the dealer, whoever he was. Great. So I'd even more to worry about and less people to look after me. Story of my life.

CHAPTER FIFTEEN

Invisible Jonno

Sometimes my dad let me help put the chips in all the wee paper bags. That way they were ready to put in newspaper when someone bought them. He never let me take the chips out of the fat, even though I was nineteen and a half. The fat was so hot that if you touched it by accident, it would peel your skin off. So I didn't mind that I wasn't allowed to do that job. I tried to get as many chips in the wee bags as I could without spilling any on the counter. My dad said I was good at it. I was also good at counting up the money at the end of the night. I counted up a lot of money, but we weren't millionaires. A millionaire is when you have more than a million pounds. I told Dad I didn't think we'd ever make that, and he told me to be quiet. He did that a lot.

I liked that girl who came into the shop sometimes. She was called Lizzy. I still liked her even when she smelled of cigarettes. I didn't like smoking, but my dad told me that sometimes I had to make exceptions. Exceptions is when you let someone do something that you wouldn't let other people do. Like when he let me read my book while we were eating breakfast. He wouldn't have let anyone else do that and so I was the exception.

Lizzy smiled at me and talked to me. Most people didn't even look at me, even when I shouted something out loud in the shop.

Sometimes it was like I wasn't there or I was invisible. Invisible is when no one can see you. But Lizzy always saw me. One day I told her about fossils, and she looked very interested. Then I told her I wanted to be a paleontologist and she didn't even say I was stupid or that I shouldn't think those things. My dad laughed, I heard him. But Lizzy looked very serious and did not laugh at all and said that it was a good idea. If I was in charge of the chips, I'd give them all to her for free.

It was very hot in the shop and I often felt sticky. Dad said that I was hot blooded, and when I told him that it was because I was a mammal and not a crocodile or other cold-blooded reptile, he said I should be quiet. I hoped that one day me and Lizzy would be married and I wouldn't have to be quiet all the time because she liked listening to what I had to say. There were two things I needed to do before I asked her to marry me. The first thing was that I had to wait until she was an adult. An adult is when you are over eighteen years old. Lizzy told me she was nearly thirteen, so I had to wait six years, which seemed like a long time but worth the wait and it gave me a chance to save up for a ring in a box. I looked at them in the window of H.Samuel and they cost more than a hundred pounds. The second thing I had to do was make sure that the man with the hat didn't ask her first because in marriage it's first come, first served. I saw this man watching her lots of times. He usually wore a furry hat with flaps that covered his ears, and when it was warmer, he wore a cap with a peak to shield his eyes from the sun. He must have had very sensitive ears and eyes.

The man with the hat watched Lizzy from far away. Lots of times, when I was in the High Street getting the messages, I saw him watching her. I didn't like the man with the hat, and I could say that because he once came into the shop and wasn't very nice. He was one of those people who acted like I was invisible. He came in with Lizzy's mum, who was always nice to me like Lizzy was. Like mother like daughter, my dad always said, which wasn't proper

English. I didn't tell him that because I didn't want to have to be quiet again.

That night, Dad was out the back getting more fish out of the boxes and so I got two bags of chips and said how much they were, all properly. Lizzy's mum said, "Thanks, Jonno" to me, and I said, "You're welcome" back. The man with the hat said he didn't want them wrapped up in newspaper, and while he said that, he looked at the counter. He had a funny look on his face and pushed on her elbow so that she walked over to the till instead of stopping and talking to me. He put the money down on the counter and pushed her elbow again so that she turned around and then he opened the door to let her out quickly. My dad came out when they'd gone and was proud of me that I'd given the chips and got the money, even though it wasn't in the till yet; it was just on the counter where the man with the hat left it. He asked me who had come in, but I couldn't speak because I was upset and sat down again to read my book.

That was the other reason why I didn't like the man with the hat. If he married Lizzy, he would try to boss her around and push her elbow, but I if married her, I would just be nice. I had five years to make sure she knew that he was bad and that I wasn't. That was a challenge as my dad said that women sometimes liked to do the opposite of what you asked them to do. So I was afraid to ask her to do anything. If I asked her not to marry him, she might marry him because she felt like doing the opposite of that. And if I told her she should marry him, she might marry him because she didn't feel like doing opposites that day. It was very confusing and made my head hurt. Maybe it was best to keep quiet like my dad said.

CHAPTER SIXTEEN

Lauren Looks in

I'm just about holding on. Still looking down at my pathetic body, which is not moving at all now except for my chest lifting up and down half-hearted. I've no strength left. Cracked lips, so dry, I feel like I could do with drinking Loch Lomond. If I could get myself up, I'd run to a river and jump in it, open my mouth and let it sink in. What was that poem we had at school, the one about water, water, everywhere? Can't think. It was something about a ship.

The lights are burning on me. My skin is still dead white and I should be sweating, but I'm not. I've nothing to sweat, no water left in my body. I don't want to be alive. I want to sleep now and not wake up. I can't stand to see myself like this, alone and helpless, starved and rotting.

I need to see Lizzy. I hope she's with Maureen. I didn't realize until now how much I rely on having my sister around. She's my only family, really. I do a lot to help her and she tries to help me back, but I don't let her. That's just me, always too independent.

Is this about me as well? Do I attract evil? Maybe this is all my fault, my own doing. Oliver. His shining eyes turned dull and his charm disappeared once he had me where he wanted me. He's a psychopath, an animal. When I die, I want him to die too. I've known him for such a short time and now this. At least Rob had the decency to get to know me first, even marry me, for Christ's sake.

There I go, making out that Rob did something right. I'm an idiot, a doormat. I can't see things that are right in front of my face.

——◆——

"You're a fat cow. Look at the state of you."

"I'm pregnant. What do you expect?" I was lying on the sofa, watching telly and eating a scone.

"Only just. You weren't this fat when you were up the duff with Lizzy."

"Keep your voice down. I don't want her to find out yet. It's too early."

"Not too early to stop stuffing your fat puss, is it?" He kicked my feet.

I said nothing.

"Did you hear what I said?" He was shouting now. "Get up, you lazy arse."

He pulled at my legs. Didn't know his own strength. I fell off the sofa completely, landed awkwardly on the carpet. The side of the coffee table knocked my belly and that was the end of that. When the ambulance came, I heard him telling them I'd been asleep and had fallen onto the floor. Aye, because that happens all the time.

It was going to be a boy. I named him Bobby.

CHAPTER SEVENTEEN

Lizzy in the Wardrobe

I decided I'd better go home and water Mum's yucca plant again, before it went all brown and withered. She loved that plant, crap knows why. It wasn't very pretty, with its spikes and jaggedy stem, but I didn't want it to get ruined all the same. Auntie Maureen said not to bother, which wasn't very nice. She never came with me back to our house, not that I'd want her to. It was better being there on my own.

I went to the flower shop and bought some purple irises. They were Mum's favourite, and I thought it would be lovely if she came home and found them on the kitchen table in a vase. She'd know straight off that I had always believed she'd come back.

It had been less than a week since I'd left home, but it seemed like forever. The house reeked of dust and old furniture. Usually it smelled of washing powder and burned toast and Mum's hairspray, all friendly. You might think a house has a smell, but it doesn't. It's the people in it that make it. After I watered the plant and then put the flowers in water, I sat in Mum's bedroom for a while and got her jewellery box out of the chest of drawers. It was one of those wooden ones with the ballerina inside, except it didn't work anymore. When you opened the lid, the ballerina just stood there and didn't twirl around like she was supposed to.

Mum didn't really have much, but I loved her jewellery. She said I could get my ears pierced for my thirteenth birthday and I could borrow her earrings. She had loads of really cool ones, all colours. My favourite thing was a silver necklace with a Scottish cross on it. It used to be Granny Mac's. Mum wore it all the time, and I'd seen her touching it with her fingertips a lot before she disappeared. It wasn't in the box, so she must have been wearing it that night. There was another one, silver with a green stone, that she wore to parties sometimes. I put on the necklace and sat at the dressing table to see what I looked like. I was quite grown-up sat there, brushing my hair and smoothing down my eyebrows, the green stone sparkling away. I put some of her lipstick on, the pale pink one. The bright red one wasn't there.

Mum always said I looked like an angel, but I thought I looked a bit weird. I wasn't anything like her; I took after my dad. My left eye was a bit smaller than my right one and my hair got all fuzzy at the ends. It looked better when she'd plaited it or tied it up for me, but I wasn't so great at doing it myself. I didn't dare ask Auntie Maureen because she always seemed too busy to brush her own hair, let alone do mine. I'd just put it in a ponytail and there were lots of wee bits that stuck out over my ears.

There was a photo of me on the bedside table. It was in a silver frame that Granny Mac bought Mum for her birthday one year. I was about five years old in the picture, sitting on the floor cross-legged, and holding a huge ice cream. There was ice cream all over my face, on my hands, and down my dress. Mum thought it was dead funny. Things were simple then.

I laid on her bed for a while, just staring at the photo. Then I remembered the wardrobe. It was really old and made of oak or something like that. It might have been Granny Mac's, but I wasn't sure. It had little legs on it and it was dead small. For some reason my mum was really protective of it; she never let me near it and sometimes she'd even lock it with a wee key if she was going out and leaving me on my own. I knew this because I'd tried to look in the wardrobe loads of times before, usually on a Friday night when she was down the social club.

I felt dead guilty, but I got up then and tried to open the doors. They were locked. I realized the last time she locked it, she was going out for the night. That night. It got me thinking that she might have hidden the key somewhere in the house rather than risk losing it. If she got steaming drunk and it was in her bag, then who knew where it would end up. I looked in all her drawers, feeling carefully around the edges and underneath her clothes. I checked under the mattress and in her pillowcase but didn't find it. She was always fiddling around in the kitchen and had two pots, one for twenty-pence pieces and one for paper clips and stuff. Sure enough, there it was amongst the coins; I don't know why I didn't think of it before. Maybe I'd never wanted to find the keys so badly.

My heart was going. What was in there? I opened the wardrobe doors quick, before I could think about it too much. At first I was a bit disappointed because all I could see was clothes hanging up and a few pairs of shoes in the bottom, a bit dusty. The clothes were ones that she wore all the time, mostly shirts and jeans. The only posh thing she had was her wedding dress, and she gave that to the charity shop after Dad left. I had a look through to the back and then found a biscuit tin, a big round one, behind her shoes. I realized that it must have been what she didn't want me to find. I pulled it out and sat on the floor; rested my hands on the top of the lid. Should I open it? I hesitated for a minute, but then I thought, well, when am I going to get another chance to have a look?

On top were two packets of photos, all of me, Mum, and Granny Mac. Some were of the three of us together, some with just two of us, and some of us on our own. None of Dad or anyone else. There was a dead brilliant one of Granny Mac holding me when I was a baby. She was looking at the camera and I was laughing and holding onto her nose. Another one had me on Mum's lap and Mum on Granny Mac's lap. We were fair nearly squashing her and we were all laughing in it. I'd never seen any of them before. I didn't know why Mum would want to hide them from me. Underneath those were some postcards, all from Granny Mac in the days when she used to go to Blackpool for her holidays. She loved Blackpool, so she did. The cards all had cartoons on the front, of nurses in short dresses and guys with red noses. The backs were all written in green ink, really short, things like, *Having a braw time, Sitting on a deck chair the noo,* or *Wish you were here.* She used to go every year with her three best friends, all of them the same age as her, all on their own having lost their husbands over the years. I wondered what had happened to them, if they were still alive and went to Blackpool without Granny Mac. That wouldn't be right.

Underneath the photos was a square white envelope and inside that were two more baby photos. They were those black-and-white ones that pregnant women get before the baby's born. I'd seen one before when Auntie Maureen was pregnant with wee Noah. Written on the back of one was *Lizzy, 21 weeks,* and on the back of the other was *Bobby, 13 weeks.* I sat and thought for a while about who Bobby was; I'd never heard of him. Then I got to thinking maybe he was my wee brother but that he was never actually born. Mum had been to the hospital quite a few times over the years, usually because she was beaten up or something was broken, so I wouldn't have realized if she had been sick or lost a baby. Poor Mum. No wonder she never wanted to talk about having another one. Did Auntie Maureen know? Did Dad even know?

I put the photos back in the envelope, careful to put them the right way around like I found them, and piled everything else back in the tin. Grown-ups never tell you anything.

When I got back to Auntie Maureen's, I did a test. I caught her off-guard, while she was at the kitchen table with her feet up on a chair. She was trying to drink a cup of tea without spilling it over one of the kids zipping around her.

"Auntie Maureen, who's Bobby?"

"Bobby? You mean Uncle Bobby, our Jimmy's cousin?"

"No, a baby. One that died."

"I don't know of a baby called Bobby, or one that died for that matter. Why? What are you talking about?"

"Oh, nothing."

I watched her face, her eyes, when I asked her, and she looked blank. I could always tell when Mum or Auntie Maureen was telling fibs because they went a bit red and looked slightly to the side of my face. So she didn't know about Bobby then. It must have been Mum's secret. I felt a bit guilty for knowing, but sad for her at the same time. I felt sad for me as well, for not having a brother and all, but that was just me being selfish.

"I watered the yucca plant. It was brown."

"That's good," she said, not really listening.

She gave me Kai to entertain while she took Kane to the loo. Kai looked at me with a cheeky grin on his wee face. I chubbed his cheeks and blew a raspberry at him and he giggled. Wee Noah was sitting in his baby swing watching us, and I could swear that he smiled as well. Kai's giggles were infectious. Auntie Maureen came back and threw herself on the sofa. Her belly and her boobs wobbled about like they had a mind of their own.

"I could put a cartoon on the telly if you want," she said. She grabbed the remote control and the boys sat down on the floor, right next to each other, looking so alike it was scary.

"Go put the kettle on, will you, Lizzy."

⋙⬥⋘

I wanted my mum. I needed her back so badly. I just couldn't stay there with Auntie Maureen for much longer. She didn't really want me there, I could tell. She didn't expect me to be staying so long; I reckoned she thought it would just be the one night or a

Nondescript Rambunctious

couple at the most. Uncle Brian didn't want me there either; he just grunted at me when he got in from work and then switched the telly on. It was like I didn't really exist, except for when I was there to entertain one of the boys. I was this thing that they didn't know what to do with. If they didn't talk to me that much, then maybe I would go away. Maybe that was why Auntie Maureen was always calling everyone to try and find out what had happened to my mum. She just wanted me away.

That was a full week I'd had off school, and I was going to go back on the Monday. I tried to look on the bright side. I'd be out of the house in the day, so I wouldn't be under Auntie Maureen's feet all the time and at least I'd be able to talk to Molly at break time and lunch and even see Simon if he was in school. That was if he wasn't away working with his mum's new schemie boyfriend. I could just imagine what this Roy guy looked like. I pictured one of those eighties mullets, all greasy at the back of his neck, and yellow fingers from smoking. A right skiver who still listened to Big Country and wore shirts tucked into jeans. With no belt. Gross.

Sometimes I wondered if my mum had gone away because of me. When she came back, I would be really good. I wouldn't talk to Simon if she didn't want me to. I wouldn't even look at him. I'd go and get her fish suppers every day if she wanted. And make her cups of tea whenever she wanted one. I would. I wouldn't see my dad, not even at Christmas, and I'd never talk about him again. Nothing else was as important as she was. Not to me. I lay in bed at night and pressed my hands together, eyes screwed shut. I didn't believe in God, but I prayed to somebody, somewhere.

Please come back.

Please don't leave me.

Please don't be dead.

CHAPTER EIGHTEEN

Oliver's Comparisons

Day 4, Tues 20 Nov: Dark urine continues to be passed in tiny amounts. Lauren has been crying, but there have been no tears due to dehydration. Thirst is now excessive and pleas for water have become more urgent although often unintelligible. Skin is bagging and flesh is decreasing. Hair is excessively greasy.

⟶•⟵

It was incredible what I could get away with. In a world of extreme technological advances, in the midst of a digital revolution, when we could send photographs using our mobile phones and clone human cells, so much evil could so easily escape the eyes of the law. I could do whatever I liked in my own home, and no one knew. All it took was an underground room, some insulation and camouflage, and a well thought-out website. It had worked for me for years, and I was confident that my methods would continue to work until we could all fly to the moon in our cars. It's easy to hide on the web, much easier than you might think.

⟶•⟵

Day 5, Wed 21 Nov: Urine output and sweating have almost ceased altogether. Extreme fatigue has set in with symptoms of confusion and disorientation. Eyes appear sunken and glazed.

≻⊷≺

I needed a break from watching Lauren and sat down to read the *Times* newspaper, feet up on the conservatory windowsill, glass of chilled Chardonnay in one hand. That day there were some excellently gruesome stories, and I wanted to sit and soak them up.

There were three reports that I thought most people would find disturbing. A woman had spent twelve years locked in the house of a psychopath. He had abducted her at the age of five and kept her like a pet in one of his bedrooms. She had no contact with anyone except him during her imprisonment and finally escaped the house at the age of seventeen, severely affected by her plight. Her family was delighted by their reunion but unbearably appalled at what had happened to her. The abductor took a gun to his neck before he could be found and arrested.

Meanwhile, in Germany, two gothic teenagers executed a high-school massacre, killing seven of their peers and injuring another five. They opened fire during assembly, using shotguns that one of them had acquired from his father's hunting collection. Their town was in mourning with a mass funeral planned for later that week.

The third story that caught my attention was about a major child-pornography ring that had been uncovered in East London, with three men arrested. One of the investigators said he had never seen such sickening images as those he found when he searched the property of the ringleader.

As I drained my glass of wine and took in those three accounts, I felt I had seen them before; they seemed strangely familiar. I realized that it was because things like that happened all the time. Another sick abduction, more teenage killers, a new child-pornography scandal. The world was full of violence and terror, and it couldn't be just me who felt unsurprised about the contents of the news. Everyone's worst nightmares had become everyday reading. And the people in the stories were the ones who'd been unlucky—they had been caught in the act or so consumed with anger, they had committed murder in front of the world.

What about all the others? The ones who hadn't been caught? Like me.

What I did, in my small world of visual experimentation, paled in comparison. I would not touch a child. I would not perform mass murder. I was just one of many small-town killers with a personal need to fulfill. In the grand scheme of things, it wasn't so wrong.

———◆———

Day 6, Thurs 22 Nov: Skin has somewhat shrivelled and lacks elasticity. Delirium has begun with periods of unconsciousness. Speech is no longer understandable. The few words spoken are about unrelated subjects. Eyes remain closed.

———◆———

The police came to my door again, and this time they weren't just lowly officers. A Detective Inspector Harry Roberts came with his sidekick, so I knew that things were getting more serious. I had been expecting them to come, because I had found out earlier they were doing the rounds. When I went to get my paper across the road, Bottle Blond was flushed with excitement because she had encountered the inspector first thing in the morning. She appeared to have an infatuation, although it hardly meant that the man would have great charm and charisma. The girl is not exactly discerning.

When DI Harry Roberts arrived at my doorstep, I found him to have mediocre looks, although he was well dressed, with an air of self-importance. Perhaps women found that attractive. I found it an irritation. He was wearing a raincoat with a cape, the sort that might be used as the costume for an inspector in a predictable ITV drama, and his shoes were the kind that needed to be shined on a regular basis because they were so cheap. Perhaps he would be even more predictable, with an alcohol problem and an ex-wife who spent all his money. Oh yes, and of course, a female sidekick who was more masculine than him.

Lauren was going through long periods of silence, and it was the physical deterioration that was getting more interesting and intense rather than the reactions and sounds. I knew there was no danger of the inspectors hearing anything, not that much noise escaped even at the loudest of times. I was calm, and had no qualms about letting DI Harry Roberts and his scrawny-looking assistant through the door and into my conservatory. They didn't stay that long in any case. Both looked at me suspiciously for a while and asked very much the same questions as the two previous officers had done. It seemed there had been reservations about me in the community because I was new in the area, and as we all know, small-town folk don't always like strangers appearing in their midst. I commented about this and the DI nodded in agreement.

"You seem like an observant man," he said.

"I try to be. It's hard being a new face."

He asked me if he could look around the house and I didn't want to arouse suspicion so I agreed. Walking slowly around the cottage, he lingered in my bedroom, glancing in my direction periodically. I assumed he wanted to see if I was looking nervous in any way. I wasn't.

"And this is your bedroom, sir?"

"Yes, this is mine. The other bedroom I use as an office, as you can see."

"You don't have many guests coming to stay?"

"No," I said. *Other than my special guests in the cellar.*

"And what work is it you do?"

"Web-based copywriting and editing. It means I can work from home most of the time."

"You are incredibly tidy," he noted, "and a minimalist sort of chap. You haven't been here long, have you? Where did you come from?"

"I came from Glasgow. Things didn't work out with my relationship. I needed to get away, if you know what I mean," I said and rolled my eyes in a way that said, "Women, you can't live with them."

"I know exactly where you're coming from. With a wife, a live-in mother-in-law, and three daughters, sometimes I feel like escaping, too," he said.

⊰⊱

That night I saw something else in my newspaper, a small article I had overlooked. I always skimmed through the stories one last time before I threw my papers away so that I didn't miss anything, and I was glad I did. A piece of research performed at Birmingham University had found that women often had a higher propensity than men for violent thoughts and intentions. It had something to do with their hormone fluctuations. It was the overall execution of the aggressive intent that was lower than men's, so in the long run, women appeared to be less violent. Anything to do with research and experimentation interested me, but the content I found captivating.

Violence is almost expected of men; it's in our blood. But when a woman does something evil, society becomes so outraged that she becomes a celebrity. Myra Hindley, the Moors Murderess; Rose West, the serial killer; Beverly Allitt, the Angel of Death;

and not forgetting our very own Queen Mary I, who burned at the stake everyone she could get her hands on. These women are a fascination, almost admired for their physical strength and psychological stamina. Why are they any different? Because rather than simply voicing their violent thoughts and intentions or writing them down like most passive-aggressive women, they had followed through on them.

Helen was one of those rare women and could easily earn celebrity status in the realm of feminine evil. I was proud to call her one of my subscribers and often wondered what she was doing in her own underground world. I should imagine something far worse than I.

CHAPTER NINETEEN

Jonno Shouts But Can't Be Heard

A policeman came in the shop. He wasn't wearing a blue uniform, but he did have shiny shoes and a badge that he showed to Dad. This was to prove who he was and to make us answer his questions.

I was at the counter doing the chips, but my dad told me to sit down at my table while he talked to the policeman. I asked the policeman if he would like some chips, but he didn't answer. My dad told him to just ignore me. He was ignoring me anyway, so he didn't need to be told. I sat down at the table with my encyclopedia, but I could easily hear them.

First of all, the policeman told my dad that he was investigating the disappearance of Lauren Finning. Investigating is when you're trying to find out about something. Lauren Finning was Lizzy's mum, and I liked both of them so I decided to listen.

He asked lots of questions about them. It was hard not to shout out the answers because I was good at that. But every time I shouted one out, I was told to be quiet or to wait a minute.

First, he asked if Dad had seen Lauren Finning with anyone other than Lizzy before she disappeared. I shouted out, "The man with the hat." The policeman was sitting with his back to me, and he didn't turn around.

Second, he asked if Lauren Finning had been in the shop much before she disappeared. I shouted out, "She did. Yes, she did."

"Just a minute, Jonno," my dad said and showed me the palm of his hand. That means stop.

Third, he asked if we'd seen anyone unusual around the town. I thought the man with the hat was very unusual. Unusual means not like anyone or anything else. He was always watching Lizzy and pushing her mum's elbows, and I didn't like him one bit. I shouted out, "The man with the hat" again, and this time neither my dad or the policeman answered back at all.

I opened up my encyclopedia and looked up global warming. No one was interested in my answers and so I thought I'd just read instead. Global warming is when everyone on the planet uses too much petrol and all the ice starts melting and making the rivers bigger. The policeman wouldn't have known about that either. He had one of those big SUV cars parked outside, and it was way too big for him. He didn't seem to know much, by the sounds of things.

CHAPTER TWENTY

For Auld Lang Syne

It's all coming to an end. I can't hang on anymore. I'm floating, weightless. Maybe I'm already dead.

Granny Mac. Mum, when I think of you now, it's your laugh that sticks in my mind. It was so infectious it would make me giggle, even if I didn't know what was funny. I can just hear it now; I would smile if I could bring myself to. You had some wee sayings that no one says much anymore. That square of chocolate was *Just to taste ma mooth*. In my birthday cards, you would always write *Lang may yer lum reek*. And my favourite of all when I was a bairn: *Dinnae spend it all at once*, as you pressed a coin into my adoring hand. You may not know this, but I wore your Scottish cross necklace all the time, right up until now. I don't think I'm still wearing it anyway. I can't feel it, but then I can't feel anything anymore. I've always loved to imagine you watching over me, but not anymore. No one would want to see this.

———◆———

Lizzy, if you can hear me, I'm sorry. If only I could be back with you; I wouldn't care if you had leaves in your hair or you smelled of satsumas or liked a boy. None of that would matter. Why would it? I'd just be there for you when you needed me. I'm your mother. I won't leave you. You're my wee angel, and you don't deserve to be alone. I'll watch over you just like Granny Mac watched over me. Please never forget the sound of my voice, the smell of my hair, the feel of my hand on your face. How much I loved you.

CHAPTER TWENTY-ONE

Lizzy Cuts Her Teens

I knew she was dead, because I felt her go. It happened when I was lying in bed one night in my room. It was beginning to feel even more like mine and not the baby's room at all. Auntie Maureen let me put a few posters up, and she finally took Noah's cot out and put all his toys downstairs so she didn't have to keep coming in for his things. She said I needed some space. I didn't bring any of my pictures from home; I got new ones from Derek's Pop-In, a wee shop on the High Street that sold cheap stuff for under a pound. I got one of The Cure and one of Joy Division because I was getting into that kind of music, moving away from boy bands and chart crap. I just didn't like all that fake blues and gangsta rap that a lot of them at school were into; it was dead boring. Indie music had soul. The shop also had candles shaped like skulls for twenty pence, and I got one of them as well; it was nice to have a bit of soft light when I couldn't sleep. When I was just staring at the walls.

Sometimes I could lie for hours, just thinking about stuff in a kind of half sleep. That night I was remembering how me, Mum, and Granny Mac used to sit on the seawall at Portobello when we used to go and see Granny Mac's sister. Great Auntie Harriet lived right near the water, and we could walk down there twice a day if we wanted to. We'd get the biggest ice creams and all take a lick of each other's to get a wee taste. Mum would always get chocolate, I'd get strawberry, and Granny Mac would get a wacky one like bubblegum or Mexican vanilla for the hell of it. She was pure mad sometimes; she really made me laugh. I don't know why I was thinking about it, I just was. Then in my half sleep, my mum turned and looked into my eyes really intense. She pulled my face nearer until I could smell her hair spray and the chocolate on her breath. It was so real. Then she kissed me on the cheek, her lips cold from the ice cream, and smiled. My heart started going really fast and I could feel my blood pumping around my body like I'd been running or something, but I was just lying there totally still. I felt hot and my face flushed. She started fading away; she was still smiling at me, but I couldn't see her face properly. Then I went all cold and shivery, like I'd stopped running and found myself inside a fridge or something, my sweat all clammy on my skin all of a sudden. She disappeared altogether, kind of faded away, and then I felt empty inside as well as cold, not like I was hungry but like I was lost.

She was gone.

It used to be me, Mum, and Granny Mac, the three of us always together. Then it was just me and Mum, and that was cool, too. Then it was just me.

Christmas and Hogmanay went by in a daze, and nothing felt the same because they weren't there. I saw my dad but just for the day. He travelled up to Dalbegie to see me like he always did; I never saw his house. The thing was he didn't stay at the bed and breakfast like he usually did; he drove back straightaway like he couldn't wait to get away from me. He knocked at the door and Auntie Maureen hid herself away in the kitchen. She couldn't bear to look at him she was still so pissed off about what he did to Mum over the years. We went out for the day, over to Inverness and mostly drove around because it was raining. It was one of those grey days when it didn't ever seem to get light; it just started off dark and ended up dark. The only good bit was that we got to talk about stuff because we were just locked up in the car together, even if it was mostly about nothing. I think he was trying to say he was sorry about Mum, but he couldn't quite bring himself to say those words exactly. As we pulled into the car park at McDonald's, he turned and actually looked at me, which was something.

"Looks like she's not coming back," he said.

"I don't know, Dad. Do you think she's dead?"

"No," he said quickly. "Well, we don't know, do we?"

"Will I have to stay at Auntie Maureen's?"

"I think that might be best, my wee darling, until we know for sure what's happened."

"And then what?"

"Then we'll have to see. You'll miss all your friends and school if you have to move down with me, won't you?"

"Not really."

"Aye, well, we'll see."

And that was it, our attempt at serious conversation, probably for another year. I didn't want to live with him and that woman. I was just testing him, but I knew where I stood and it hurt.

━━◆◆◆━━

A few weeks after I got that letter from Simon, I went round to his place, I couldn't wait any longer. I had to see Roy for myself and find out what was going on, why I'd not seen Simon. I listened at the door for a wee while and couldn't hear anyone, so I knocked quietly just in case Simon's mum was in her bed as usual. I wasn't expecting anyone to answer, so I was that shocked when the door opened and there was this Roy guy standing there in his pants. Dead baggy they were, with holes where the waistband was coming away. I was right about the mullet, but it wasn't black. He had cheap-looking streaks, with brown roots that were too long. He was all peely wally, and skinny, with red spots on his chest.

"What is it?" he said, and some spit flew in the air that just missed me.

"Is Simon in?"

"Aye, who are you?"

"Lizzy."

He turned around and shouted down to the kitchen. "Simon! It's your wee girlfriend here, Lizzy. Are you in?"

I heard his mum huffing upstairs at the noise. Simon appeared with half of his head shaved, looking pissed off.

"What's going on?" I stepped inside.

Roy was grinning. "He's had nits; fucking Nitty Nora sent him home from school, so she did." He pushed Simon back into the kitchen, and I followed them in. Simon sat down on a chair and folded his arms. There was dry hair all over the floor.

"I didn't have nits," he said.

"So you did, you wee scabby fuck. I saw one of them fly off your head and onto the table. It was disgusting. Let's get the rest of that mop off the now." Roy grabbed the electric shaver and started with the rest of Simon's hair. I stood and watched, not really sure what to do.

"You didn't tell me you had such a gorgeous fucking girlfriend, Simon," he said.

"She's not my girlfriend."

"Why the hell not? She's fucking gorgeous, so she is," he said.

He looked me up and down a couple of times and kept staring at my chest. It made me feel dead self-conscious, as I'd started to develop in that area, and I didn't have the courage to ask Auntie Maureen to buy me some bras. I thought she'd probably laugh at me.

"She's not even thirteen, leave her alone," said Simon.

"You should get in there, laddy. I was twelve when I lost my cherry, to the fucking babysitter no less. She was gagging for it and all."

"Aye, right," said Simon.

"That's enough, you cheeky fuck." Roy slapped Simon on his forehead really hard. I watched as a red mark came up; you could see the fingers. He finished shaving and stood back to check he hadn't missed any hairs. His pants were drooping down at the back and showing his crack. I pulled a face behind his back and Simon nearly laughed. I thought the shaved head made Simon look dead cool. I hadn't noticed his eyelashes before, but they were really dark and long. He had good skin as well, not like a lot of the spotty boys at school. He really suited having no hair. He'd got a good-shaped head, not a peanut or a flathead. I went a bit red for looking at him; I could feel my cheeks go all hot.

"What do you think, blondie?" said Roy.

"I hate to say it, but I think you've done him a favour."

"There you go, scabby heid, I've done you right. You'll be getting your leg over now, right enough," said Roy. He laughed and coughed at the same time, spitting on the floor. I was right; he had to be the worst boyfriend of Simon's mum's ever.

"Can I go out now?" asked Simon.

"Aye, get out of my sight for a bit. I'm away back to my bed," said Roy.

We left in a hurry, leaving all the mess, before he changed his mind. I was dead shocked that Simon had asked Roy if he could go out, like he was his dad or something. I'd never heard Simon ask if he could do anything; he just did stuff. We ran down to the river and sat in our old place. Simon had some ciggies but no whisky. Sometimes he got Smirnoff Ice, which was really nice, but he'd been in a rush to get out. I asked him if he was scared of Roy and he said he wasn't, but I didn't believe him. I could still see that red mark on his forehead, and he kept touching it and wincing.

After the head-shaving incident, things got a lot worse, but Simon didn't really talk about it. A cigarette burn on his arm, cuts on his legs, raised yellow bruises on his face, a broken nose. It was like he was getting beaten but didn't want to admit it because I'd think he was a sissy or something. It was dead silly, but that's what boys were like sometimes; they wanted to be the big man. The stuff he did tell me was more about the way Roy made him run messages all the time. He made him pick up and drop off packages all over the place. Sometimes he had to get the bus all the way to Inverness. At first he argued and refused, but after a wee while, he knew it wasn't worth it. He didn't even know what was in the packages and didn't dare open them up because they were wrapped up so carefully it would be dead obvious if he touched them. Sometimes they were really heavy and Simon reckoned that they were guns that he was carrying about. I reckoned some of them were drugs, wrapped in brown packages like I saw on *The Bill* sometimes. If Simon got caught with one by the police, he'd be in big trouble, and we guessed that was why Roy didn't want to do his deliveries himself. What a skank.

I hadn't been seeing Molly that much; apparently her mum thought I had become a bad influence. That was a joke because Molly was the one who always wanted to skive off school. The reason she thought I was bad was because I'd been hanging out with Simon more, and he looked and acted dead rough. She'd seen me about the town with him and didn't like it, probably thought we might turn Molly into a drug addict or something like that. Or make her have a tattoo like the one Simon had done on his arm, aye, right. Molly kept on telling her mum that me and Simon were cool, but she wasn't having any of it. I reckoned if my mum was still around, she'd be the same way. It was because they didn't really know Simon. They thought he was a bit wild anyway, then he got his head shaved and got the tattoo, so of course he turned into some kind of mobster in their eyes. All of a sudden I couldn't go round to Molly's after school and Molly wasn't allowed out except at the weekends. Simon was all I had most of the time and that was okay because I was all he'd got, too. He had his own problems to tell me, what with Roy on the scene, and of course I had mine to tell him.

It was my birthday in March. I turned thirteen but I wasn't excited about it, not really. Dad sent me a card with a tenner in it and wrote "Love Dad" inside, that was all. Simon got me a wee bottle of whisky, and we shared it down at the river after school; it was dead cool. In the evening, Auntie Maureen bought me a cake and some pink candles, and we all sat around the kitchen table to eat it, even Uncle Brian. Kai and Kane sang "Happy Birthday" and everyone clapped. It was nice of them, but I burst into tears, I couldn't help it. I ran to my bedroom and hid in there for the rest of the night. Auntie Maureen knocked on the door and asked if I was all right, and I just said I was okay and that I wanted to be on my own. She just left me, didn't argue or come in to stroke my hair like Mum would have done. I heard them all downstairs, finishing up and chattering like they'd forgotten what the cake was even for.

After that I had a few more wobblers, but everyone said it was to be expected given that they hadn't found my mum and no one knew anything else about what happened to her. The more gossip I heard around the town, the more stupid it sounded and the more down I felt about it all. It was like no one really cared; they just got off on the misery of it all. All I really knew for sure was that she went for a Chinese with a man the week before she disappeared. Of course the police interviewed everyone who worked at the restaurant, but none of them remembered anything significant.

Molly dragged me down there one Saturday to make a few of

Nondescript Rambunctious

our own investigations, but we didn't get anywhere. The owner of the restaurant didn't speak very good English, and we could hardly understand a word he was saying. His wife was better and she told us that there was no way they would remember a particular customer on a particular night just from a photo. She was quite nice to us, but she'd obviously been through it all loads of times before. I'd never been in the Chinese; it was dead funny. They had a fake waterfall going down one of the walls with Christmas-tree lights around it. When we left, Molly took a handful of boiled sweets out of the jar at the front desk. They tasted like old socks, so they did; she shouldn't have bothered.

—◆◆—

The summer arrived and things seemed different. There was a new smell in the air; it was like the start of a new life without my mum. People wore short sleeves even though it really wasn't that hot, and Jessica in the newsagents got her white legs and horrible strappy sandals out again. She must have had those things for years; they were dead grubby and she looked like trash in them. She sprayed something in her hair to make it more blond, but it always ended up yellow.

Wee Noah started to walk, not very well, but he grabbed hold of everything in sight and fell on his arse a lot, bless him. The twins went off to nursery so Auntie Maureen was supposed to have more time for everything else, not that the house was ever tidy or clean. I did my bit, but I couldn't tidy up after everyone all the time. Sometimes I felt like the resident slave, I did that much cleaning for her. Uncle Brian said I was a godsend, but I knew he was lying to make me feel more wanted there. I hated the fact that everyone was getting on with their lives as if nothing had happened, and I was left wondering what the hell I was going to do. I had at least three years left of school and five years until I was eighteen, when I could do what I wanted, so that meant that I was going to live like a housekeeper with people that didn't want me for what seemed like forever. Folk just got out their summer clothes, looked forward to a wee holiday if they were lucky, and ate ice cream without feeling guilty or sad or confused. And there was me feeling so miserable so much of the time. Why was everyone else happy except me? What had I done to deserve that?

——◆——

When I cut myself, I could feel the blood releasing out of my body, pulsating away from me. I did it at night when everyone else was in bed and I was on my own. It was like a pressure building up inside me through the day that I could let off, like steam. I had a pink razor that I bought out of Boots, and I used it on my arms and sometimes on my belly. It felt good on the underside of my arms, in the middle, away from my wrists. I didn't want to kill myself. I did it slowly, pulling the razor along my skin, feeling the sting of the cut only when I'd finished. It only hurt a bit, but enough to get the rush. I didn't know why I was doing it; it was just something I had to do to feel normal again.

CHAPTER TWENTY-TWO

Oliver and Repercussions

Was I a coward for trapping people, tying them down, not giving them a chance to fight back? It was something that often went through my mind when one of my bodies shut down. It was a post-murder depression, if such a thing exists. When Lauren died, I felt very flat, listless, almost reluctant to bury her. She was always going to die. It was the inevitable result of my actions, but still, it was a jolt to my existence.

Day 7, Fri 23 Nov: The body is deceased. Decay has begun prematurely and disposal should be imminent. The skin is extremely withered and yellow in colour. The chest appears almost concave, a unique finding to date. Number eighteen seems to have quite literally collapsed in on herself.

My first memory of being called a coward was in primary school. I could only have been seven or eight years old. I had pushed over one of the older girls, and she ended up face down on the grass outside the canteen building. She had been taunting me all week, calling me "Bugsy" because in those days my teeth were far too big for my face and protruded like tombstones. She bent over and put her freckled face next to mine so I could smell orange juice on her breath. It felt unnervingly warm on my skin. Some of the others in my class had laughed and some of them hadn't, but nevertheless she had humiliated me in front of everyone. I stopped her from chanting the only way I knew how, and she had fallen hard, skirt thrown up to her waist, face down. She cracked one of her teeth on a stone, and she started to cry. I stood over her and stared blankly, unable to think of anything clever to say. The next thing I knew I was a "coward" for pushing over a girl. Even though she was taller and heavier than I was; even though she had been cruel to me for days.

When Lauren expelled her last breath, squeezed out when her body collapsed, I distinctly heard that word. "Coward." Whether it was intentionally said, I do not know, but that is what I heard. Lauren was purely a victim. I had no reason for causing her pain and death, and had no motive other than my own calling. "Coward." That was just women all over. They got inside my head. I kept Lauren in the cellar for a few more days, watched her decompose until the smell became unbearable. I took less pleasure in this final stage; however, a few of my subscribers requested that I keep the cameras and lights on as long as possible. I dug a grave in the back garden and placed the body into it before piling earth and leaves on top as an extension of my compost heap. I did the work early in the morning. The space was completely private; however, I didn't want to create suspicion by making noise late at night. Why would someone be digging in his garden in the dark unless it was for an untoward reason? I liked having the compost; I added all my vegetable peelings and scraps to it; piled my raked leaves onto it. In a funny way I felt quite self-righteous in having her there, close to the earth.

I wrapped up Lauren's clothes and belongings in a bin liner and took it down to one of the more remote parts of the river. I took care to wear my gloves, as I always did when handling evidence. When she brought herself to my house that night, she was carrying only a small handbag of tan brown leather. The bag was uncluttered and pristine, like her. It contained only a hairbrush, a set of keys, her lipstick, a wallet with a clasp, and a mobile phone that was switched off. The wallet was the old-fashioned kind with a plastic compartment for photos. There was only one picture inside, of three women: Lauren, Lizzy, and an older woman who I assumed was Lauren's mother. They looked happy and oblivious to their fates, which I found at once endearing and pathetic.

When I got to the riverbank, I added some large rocks to the plastic bag, tied it up with yellow twine, and threw it into the churning water. No one would find it there.

The weeks passed with only one more visit from DI Harry Roberts. I believed I had been the subject of much discussion amongst the locals, but no one had been able to muster any good reason why I might have had something to do with the disappearance of one of their most-loved residents. He took another tour of my house and asked me the same questions one more time. It was clear that he had a hunch but couldn't quite fathom what it was about me that wasn't right. The job of a DI must rely on intuition to a certain extent, but I had behaved exceptionally well and was courteous to everyone I met in Dalbegie. He just couldn't put his finger on it. I continued with my daily visits to the newsagents, of course, and gleaned my information from Bottle Blond, who hadn't given up trying to entice me to her dull Friday night ventures at the pub. Even after knocking her back a dozen times, she mentioned it again.

"The *Times* is it? You look tired, Oliver. Have you been working too hard again?"

"Yes and yes," I said.

"You need a break; it's Friday. You should come to the pub tonight with me and the gang; we have such a giggle every week. You know what they say about all work and no play."

"No, I don't."

"Makes Jack a dull boy." She said this as if she had come up with something original that I might not have heard of before. Stupid people can't help but judge others by their own lowly standards.

"That's me," I said. I went to leave and she called after me.

"You know what else some people are saying?"

I stopped and turned back, curious to know. "And what's that?"

"That you were seeing Lauren behind our backs and that you've done her in," she said with a smirk on her face. She raised one eyebrow in what she must have thought was a sexy fashion.

"Interesting," I said. *And so true.*

"If you want to put them straight, then you'd better come out and meet some people."

"Oh, I shouldn't have to do that," I said.

I took a glimpse back in the shop after I had left and saw her scowling. It must have really irritated and perplexed her that there was a man in town who wasn't interested in going out with her. It amused me, but not enough to make her my next subject. She wouldn't exactly put up a fight on the seduction front, and, you know, I did like a challenge.

——⸎——

Life in such a small town was certainly more interesting than anywhere I'd lived before. In a city, one disappearance means nothing. An article in the local newspaper may get read and forgotten; perhaps a piece on the regional news may touch a few hearts. But for the most part, losing someone affects only the closest of friends and family. In Dalbegie, one disappearance made an impact on almost everyone. Months later, many people were still talking about it and making up stories about what they thought had happened. I overheard talk all the time, in the queue at the post office, in the grocery stores. Had she killed herself, maybe thrown herself in the river? How could she have left that wee girl behind? Perhaps her ex-husband had abducted her, jealous that she was seeing someone else. Did her new man take her away; kidnap her as a sex slave? Some of them were quite laughable. A forty-year-old sex slave, I didn't see it somehow; she should be so lucky. I hadn't seen such marked repercussions of my work before, and it felt good.

The greatest effect was of course on Lauren's daughter, who could be seen traipsing around the town with that reprobate of a boy. There was also an older man on the scene, perhaps the boy's father or stepfather. Either way, he didn't look fit to be in the company of two kids. I was no expert, but to me he looked like he was a drug user. His eyes were constantly widened with that perpetual surprised look that came with substance abuse. The boy was the one I had seen her with at the river a couple of times before. He always looked like he needed to be scrubbed from head to foot.

I followed Lizzy once or twice, and it appeared that she was living at number eighteen MacIntyre Street with a family who I assumed were relatives. The front garden was full of plastic toys, and the grass was trodden and bare. I saw a baby, a young boy, and two more toddlers come and go with their mother, at least one of them always screaming if not crying. Billy, Kai, Kane, and baby Noah, perhaps? The mother had the same hair colour and tilted nose as Lauren, but that was where the resemblance ended. It couldn't be the ideal place for a child-turned-teenager to live, and it was no wonder Lizzy had started to spend most of her time out of the house. I didn't blame her.

There was an interesting dynamic developing between Lizzy and her new friends, and I decided that I would begin to follow them. What a treat it was to be able to scrutinize a community, and no one would notice me doing it. I was careful. I could observe as lives fell apart, knowing that I was partly responsible. It was empowering to me, energizing. I felt myself lifting out of my moderately depressed state.

It was time to move on.

I started a new section at the back of my notebook, called "Repercussions." It was the first time that I'd had the luxury of observing the outcome of my work so closely, and I thought it deserved to be documented. So the section started with Experiment Number Eighteen, and I would compare wider results from there on. Not starting at number one wasn't ideal, wasn't linear, but it couldn't be helped. I couldn't reflect backwards; it didn't work like that.

My main subject was, of course, Lauren's daughter, who had fallen from nice pre-teen girl to angst-ridden adolescent within a matter of months. The physical signs were there; she had cut her long blond hair and done something to it so that it stuck out at all angles from her head. Sometimes she tied it back to reveal the shaved sides of her head. Clearly, she was trying to make some kind of statement. She reminded me a little of that blond woman who was in *The Thompson Twins* in the eighties. It amused me to see teenagers throwing themselves back in time. Of course she was a lot younger that that woman and much prettier, but the gist of the look was there. She wore lots of black makeup and sometimes painted her nails black, too. Her attire had degenerated into a scruffy urchin look, clothing often far too big for her and always black or grey. Her young male friend had got himself a tattoo, which I thought made him look rougher than ever. He probably thought it made him more attractive and manly, but he was sadly mistaken. As soon as the summer hit and the air got a little warmer, he began to show it off by wearing short-sleeve T-shirts, even though it was never really hot.

I often saw Lizzy and her friend stop at the newsagents, probably to buy cigarettes from Bottle Blonde, who must have known they were too young to be smoking. I watched both of them smoking on several occasions, often at that spot down on the riverside. It was difficult to get close enough to hear them talking because they both spoke so quietly and so seldom. I suspected that as teenagers they were far too tormented and depressed to raise their voices. They just sat there, drinking from a hip flask or straight from a liquor bottle, watching the water run past and occasionally muttering something. They never touched; they were not yet lovers, but I often wondered when something would happen between them.

The older man was never there at the riverside, and I doubted he knew about their secret meeting place. He appeared on the scene on the High Street or in McDonald's or the café, where they would mung around when they were not at the river. He was an odious specimen of a man and had badly dyed hair, cut into a spectacular mullet. Greasy strands hung limp on the back of his neck. Tall and wiry, he looked like he had been in a fight or two; his nose had been broken, and he had scars on one side of his face. Most revolting of all, he had a grotty pager attached to his belt. I hadn't seen one in years, and even then they were used by the dregs of society.

One day I saw the three of them sitting in a booth in McDonald's, and although fast food horrified me, I got myself a milkshake and sat at the next table. I pretended to read a newspaper and listened with some fascination at their juvenile banter. I quickly gathered that Lizzy's friend's name was Simon and the older man was Roy.

"I hate these chips; I like ones from the chippy." Lizzy was sulking.

"You live down that chippy; it'll do you good to have a change," said Roy.

"What, thin chips instead of fat chips? That's a big change, right enough," she said.

"Don't you be cheeky, I'll skelp you," he said. "At least there's no fucking mental case in here who'll dribble in them."

"The guy in the chippy is not a mental. He's just a wee bit slow," she said. "Jonno's all right."

"Fucking mental if you ask me, so he is. You wouldn't catch me going in there again, you don't know what you might catch. Get some fucking mental disease."

She ignored this and looked out of the window.

"What is it you want me to do then, Roy?" asked the boy, Simon.

"That's right, let's get down to some business, man to man, eh?" said Roy. "Nothing you need to bother about eh, love."

He sidled over to Lizzy and patted her knee. She moved away and scowled at him. He shrugged, gulped down his Coke and burped, making me shudder. I could smell him from where I was sitting; he stank of cheap deodorant, cigarettes, and stale alcohol. He passed something under the table to Simon.

"See this parcel? I want you to take it on the number seventeen down to Auchteragie. Get off the bus right in the centre of the town, opposite the big ScotMid there. Take a left down Canal Road and get yourself all the way down to the council estate. My man will be at the play park ,so make yourself known by sitting on one of the swings."

"Will he give me something to bring back?"

"Aye, another package. You bring it straight back, you hear? I'll be timing you, and I'll fucking kick your arse if I think you've been dallying, right?"

"You paying me for this?"

"I'll sort you, don't worry about that," said Roy.

After they left, I followed Roy. Lizzy and Simon went off to run their errand, which I decided was most likely to deliver money and pick up drugs or vice versa. I was curious to know what Roy did to keep himself busy when he wasn't bothering people younger and more naive than himself. First, he sat on a bench outside Woolworths and smoked two cigarettes in a row. All the while he watched the tips of his fingers and nodded his head as if the cigarette was some gourmet brand that tasted of something fantastic. Then he dragged himself to his feet and stood in front of the window of the electrical shop, to watch the end of a Scottish football match on television. This took about twenty minutes; much of it spent groaning out loud and kicking the ground. An elderly man stood next to him and groaned with him for a few minutes until Roy swore a little too loudly. The elderly man looked a bit startled and sloped off. After that, he took himself to the off-licence, bought a single can of Special Brew, and drank it on his way home. I assumed he lived permanently with Simon and his mother on Bamberley Drive; I'd seen them all wandering down there together. He walked slowly, dragging his feet, like a man who didn't really want to go home but didn't have a lot of choice. Every so often he would pause and take a swig of his beer, shaking his head slightly every time, his greasy hair sticking against his collar.

I had only seen Simon's mother close up once before, when she came out of the front door to chase him. She had been wearing a dressing gown and slippers and looked like she had just stepped out of bed even though it was almost three o'clock in the afternoon. She had shouted after him, brandishing a wooden spoon. "Simon, get your hairy arse back here, you fucking wee brat."

"I've got to go, Mum."

"Did you take money out of my purse? I'll fucking kill you when you get back."

"I didn't take nothing, Mum. I've got to do a message for Roy or he'll do one on me;" he had said and ran.

"I'll be checking my money, so I will, you fucking fucker," she said before retreating into the house.

She was skinny with a puffy face. Really thin, like she didn't eat food but drank plenty of alcohol to give her face that bloated look. Her straw-like hair was dyed yellow. She and Roy deserved each other, a classic white-trash couple. When Roy got to the house, he listened at the door before putting his key slowly and quietly in the lock. She probably stayed in bed all day and didn't relish being woken up. I hated Roy even more when I saw that. What a pathetic specimen of a man, tiptoeing around his woman but playing power games with children.

The worst kind.

People who dominated those much younger than themselves had to be stood up to. They needed to take a good look at themselves, and that was what I intended for Roy. No one should take advantage of kids, and if they did, they should pay for it. Setting this aside, Lizzy was my subject, living as a consequence of my actions. I did not want Roy to come in and affect the results of my experiment by forcing himself on her and making too much of an impact on her life. His sordid attempts to be some kind of dealer were for the adult world. And if he tried to touch her again, I would find it hard to restrain myself.

I stayed up until the early hours of the morning, writing in my notebook. I thought of several ways to put things straight and believed I had devised a solution that satisfied me. Roy would soon be sorry he was born.

CHAPTER TWENTY-THREE

Lizzy's First Snifter

Roy was such an arse; I so wished he'd never come on the scene. Simon hated him, but he'd no choice but to run about like a tit getting messages and bringing back fuck knows what. We talked about opening one of the packages one day but we were just too scared to actually do it. It got to the stage where me and Simon were doing a couple of runs a week, and Roy trusted us completely. We thought he was a stupid fucking eejit, that he'd regret it one day.

Simon's mum hadn't had the best track record with boyfriends, but Roy really was the biggest ned she'd ever been with. I kept saying it because it was true. She wasn't exactly God's gift, right, but I'd noticed she'd really gone downhill since he'd been around and that was saying something. She used to get out of her bed in the afternoons and tidy up the house, make tea, maybe watch a bit of telly downstairs. She'd have a bath and do her hair and go down the social or the pub a couple of nights a week. But since Roy was on the scene, she didn't appear out of her bed until teatime, and even then she looked like she hadn't slept in about a hundred years. Every time I saw her, she slurred her words and rubbed at her head like she'd forgotten where she was or what she was doing. Simon told me she hadn't been down the social for weeks.

I wondered what Roy had been doing to her or giving her to make her like that.

We often did a bunk off school and went down to the river to smoke some fags and drink the Special Brew that Simon scabbed from Roy's stash. Roy was off his box most of the time, so he never noticed when we took a couple of his cans. It was brilliant to have our wee hideout that no one knew about. The best part was that we could go down there and sit for as long as we wanted without being bothered by Roy.

That summer we were down there all the time, in the grass with our heads propped up by our hoodies. When the sun was out, it was fairly warm because our spot was well sheltered by all the bushes and weeds and stuff. As long as Roy wasn't using us, we could be there as long as we wanted. Simon's mum was in her bed all day, he'd got no dad, and Auntie Maureen couldn't really give a shit about me and what I got up to.

One day I lay sipping on the beer and I could feel the alcohol giving me an instant kick, as I'd not eaten anything much. It had been bedlam in Auntie Maureen's kitchen that morning, what with the twins throwing cereal around and Noah filling his nappy twice in a row. Uncle Brian had left for work early as usual and so we had to cope the best we could. It was dead obvious that he didn't start work at that time; he just wanted to get out of the house. So I didn't have time to get myself some toast and that was why I was getting more pished than usual. I was enjoying the water running over the wee boulders in the river. It was mesmerizing watching water; I could do it for hours on end. Sometimes I saw a fish jumping as well. It was so relaxing, and for a few minutes, I forgot everything: Mum, Granny Mac, Auntie Maureen and the boys, school, even Roy. Simon was dead quiet as well, and all I could hear was the splash of the water and the birds making their wee noises in the trees opposite. Then he leaned over and kissed me on the lips. I saw him coming, he shuffled about on his elbows,

Nondescript Rambunctious

all a bit awkward, and hovered over my face for a second. I shut my eyes so he wouldn't feel embarrassed and then it was all over in a second. He tasted of Special Brew and fags, but then again I probably did as well. Then he went back to where he was before, leaning back on his bag as if nothing had happened.

"You can kiss me again if you like," I said.

"Eh?" he said, pretending not to hear.

"You heard."

He grinned and shimmied up on his elbows again. He was dead good-looking with his new crew cut, hair grown out just a wee bit. It was kind of funny that Roy shaved his head, thinking he was being the hard man bully, but it just made Simon look brilliant. He kissed me again, this time for longer and he stuck his tongue in my mouth as well. I quite liked it really, but it wasn't what I imagined a snog was like. Molly told me she'd snogged Barry Smyth down the alley near school, and it wasn't that great because he tasted of chips and it was all a bit dribbly. I knew then what she meant. Still, it was brilliant because it was Simon and I really fancied him with his new hair and his dead cool tattoo.

We sat there for a bit longer. I think we were a bit embarrassed that it had happened and not quite sure what to do next. I said we should go get some chips because I was starving, and he got up right away. I think he was glad of something else to do. We got our stuff together, and he grabbed my hand as we walked down the bank to the pathway.

"Am I your girlfriend now, then?" I said.

"Aye, if you want."

"That's not very romantic, is it?" I said.

He just laughed at that. We walked down to the chippy without letting go of each other's hands, and they went a bit sweaty. I didn't want to be the first to break free though.

I loved the chippy; it was called Mr. Biggin's, but there was no one called Mr. Biggin, it was just a name they chose. Not that anyone called it Mr. Biggin's. It was just "the chippy" because it was the only one in town. It wasn't very big; there were only three tables at the front where you could sit inside, but then again most people got a carry-out. The tables were plastic, and they put paper tablecloths on them so they didn't even have to wipe the plastic. Kids thought they were great because they could draw on them with crayons and not get into trouble. And pished folk could spill sauce and grease everywhere, and it didn't matter. If I owned a chippy, I reckoned I'd do exactly the same thing, paper tablecloths on plastic tables, brilliant.

The guy that owned it was called Jack McNulty and he worked in there with his son Jonno. Jack McNulty did the frying and the till, and Jonno changed the paper tablecloths every once in a while and served the chips if it was busy. Otherwise, he just sat at one of the tables reading an encyclopedia. He was the guy that Roy slagged and said was mental, but he wasn't really. He was just a bit simple and spent a lot of his time with his nose in that big book learning about stuff, anything that took his fancy. Most folk got all their facts from the internet, but Jonno got his from a book and there was nothing wrong with that. My mum told me once that Jonno could understand everything perfectly well; he was just a bit slow to reply and that was so true. You could ask him a question and he'd completely ignore you for ages, then come up with the answer clear as day, just when you thought he hadn't heard you. Jack McNulty asked him questions all day, just for something to do. Sometimes it was personal stuff like what he'd like to do on Sunday, and sometimes it was factual stuff like what was the capital of Turkey or what year was America discovered. Jonno always got it right; it was amazing. I was in there once getting me and Mum's fish suppers on a Friday, and Jack McNulty asked Jonno what was 7,532 times by twelve. It was dead busy in there and Jonno was shovelling chips into a bag. He wrapped up the bag, handed it to the old dear in the queue, then said it was 90,384; all casual, like it was an easy question. I wasn't sure if anyone else noticed what was going on, but I did and I was dead impressed. I told him so as well, and he gave me a great big grin.

When I went in there with Simon after our snog, Jonno was sitting on a chair at one of the tables because it wasn't busy. He was bent right over so his face was only a few inches from a book and he was studying it really hard and mouthing the words. Simon went up to get us some chips and I sat down opposite Jonno.

"You all right, Jonno?"

He didn't look up; he was intent on finishing the bit he was reading. I waited until it looked like he'd got to the end of the page.

"Did you find out anything interesting?"

He looked at me and closed the book. "Yes, I did," he said and folded his arms.

"What was it then?"

"It was about fossils," he said.

We were almost having a conversation, which was more than I'd got out of him in all the time I'd known him.

"What about them?"

He looked at me intently and paused for what seemed like forever. I was still getting a bit of a rush in my head from the Special Brew, and his big staring eyes were making me a bit dizzy. Finally, he answered. "Fossils are the remains or imprints of plants or animals preserved from prehistoric times. The study of fossils is palaeontology. They are an invaluable record of the earth's history. After I've been in the chippy for long enough, and saved up, I'm going to be a palaeontologist."

His dad snorted at that and said, "Aye, that'll be right, son."

"That sounds brilliant," I said. "You're dead clever, so you are, Jonno."

He smiled. "I know I am," he said. "I'd go to normal school if I could."

Normal school. I felt awful then. There I was skiving off,

snogging and eating chips, and there he was wanting to go to school so desperately, having to work so hard just to be like everyone else.

"You could go to school, of course you could," I said.

He shook his head violently and went back to reading his book. His head went down and the barriers came up again. I said goodbye and went to get my chips from Simon, who was talking to Jack McNulty about some football match that was on the day before. Some guys are too normal for their own good; or predictable more like.

>—>◆<—<

Something else happened that day that I'd never done before. First I kissed Simon, then after we'd been to the chippy, we went back to his house and snorted some drugs. Roy gave us them as he said we had earned them, then threatened that if we told anyone he would skin us alive and throw us into the river. He was a real charmer when he wanted to be. The stuff he gave us was a white powder. I thought it was cocaine, and he laughed his head off and said he wouldn't waste that on us when we didn't know the difference. It was speed, which apparently was a lot cheaper. It was wrapped in a wee cardboard square, and we took it into Simon's bedroom and laid it out on one of his vinyls because that was what you did if you were cool. Simon took a fiver and rolled it up so we could snort a line of it each, and it felt dead rock and roll. We couldn't put any music on, though, because his mum was still asleep, even though it was nearly four o'clock. What a joke.

Simon went first and snorted it up in a second, then it was my turn and I felt a bit nervous, like I was going to make an arse of myself. I took the fiver and bent over, held one nostril in and hoped I wouldn't sneeze it out afterwards. I managed to do it fair easily though, a real pro. It only took a couple of minutes to kick in and I felt a rush of energy hit my insides. I looked at Simon and he sucked in his breath, eyes wide.

Nondescript Rambunctious

"Shall we go back out?"

"Let's go to the park and run," I said.

So off we went to the park and ran all the way through the playing field to the kids' swings. It was pure brilliant; it was like my blood was pumping twice as fast around my body and I forgot all my worries for the whole time. Then we sat on a couple of swings and soared through the air holding hands until it went dark. It was a great afternoon so it was. Auntie Maureen had a go at me for getting back late, but I made something up about having to stay in the school library for a project. I didn't think she believed, me but I couldn't have cared less. I hadn't felt that good since before Mum went. I didn't even need to cut myself that night; I just didn't need the release. Speed might have been cheap, but it did the trick for me; that was for sure. What a laugh.

CHAPTER TWENTY-FOUR

Oliver and the Golden Egg

There's nothing worse than taking advantage of a child. Nothing. Adults should know better than to go home with a stranger or to take drugs, but a child is inexperienced, easily influenced, searching for acceptance from those who are supposedly worldlier. To see Roy giving Lizzy and her friend drugs gave me a pain in my head. I didn't doubt that was what he was doing. I'd seen them all wandering through town with blank looks on their faces, glazed eyes and greasy hair, kicking cans into the gutter and scratching at their forearms. Lizzy looked five years older than she did at the beginning of the summer. Her eyes had black rings underneath, her hair dishevelled. That boy, Simon, got yet another tattoo. It was on his neck: a snake wrapped around halfway, cheaply done and in that dark turquoise colour. It repulsed me. I'd seen Lizzy and Simon holding hands in the street when they were alone. Roy would be at home, too drunk to leave his stinking pit I imagined; that whore of a woman clinging to him with her filthy talons. Roy deserved that stinking bitch and she deserved him. What better than an ugly tramp for such an odious specimen of a man. But Lizzy with Simon and his cheap body art? I didn't know who I felt more sorry for; it was a close call. Simon, simply because he'd been sucked into the gloom of a woman's world, or Lizzy, because she felt the need to suck in someone with no prospects, trash for a family, an increasing drug habit, and no future. So much for young love; I'd never believed in it.

I was beginning to wish I'd never started the repercussions idea because I was getting too involved. I felt anger, to the point that I wanted to get rid of all of them one by one. But I knew it wasn't exactly a sensible idea, even though none of them deserved to be on the planet.

One night I got very passionate about the very thought of destruction on a mass scale. I was drinking The Macallan 12-year-old, from a crystal glass bought as part of a set when I last visited Edinburgh. I had a measuring device and usually poured myself exactly one-eighth of an ounce; however, that night I gave up the idea of rationing after the first drink. I didn't like to dilute whisky with water, but I did like it on ice, made from filtered water of course and frozen for a minimum of two days. I enjoyed the way the ice cubes clinked against the crystal each time I picked up the glass; it was such a comforting sound when I was alone in the house without even a body in the basement for company.

The whisky seemed to heighten my senses, and I felt almost erotic that night, the lambswool blanket on my lap soft and tender, the warmth of the whisky routing its way deep into my body. The antique clock that I picked up at an auction was ticking rhythmically on the mantel, in sync with the slow pounding of my heart. My fingers trembled and the ice cubes clinked together again. I yearned for another body in the house; I wanted, needed, that power again. My drug was different to most; it was acute awareness and control that I craved, rather than escape and ecstasy. I had always waited for a decent period of months after a victim was gone, and that time was coming to an end; I could feel it washing away with the soft patter of light rain on the window. The evenings were getting longer, the days darker, and my needs stronger with every lengthening shadow. I began to think about the years gone by;

it was a time for reflection as well as anticipation of what was to come. I tried so hard to keep my father and mother out of my head, but sometimes they emerged, unwanted, as phantoms of my past.

———➤◆◄———

My father was in the Royal Navy and was therefore away from home for months at a time. I used to look forward to his return for the whole period he was away, checking the days on my wall calendar and looking up his whereabouts in my atlas. The atlas, presented to me on my eighth birthday, had always been a most treasured possession. He told me he had bought it in America, which seemed to me so distant and exotic. I kept the price sticker on the inside back cover, the amount in dollars, to prove its worldliness. In my adult years, I became rather internet obsessed, but would always consult a physical map or atlas when I travelled, the crackle of paper and folds in the pages making a journey seem tactile, somehow more personal.

Before each trip away, my father would draw with a red Biro on my atlas, marking out his route across the ocean. He would sit me down on a leather chair in his study and pull another close for himself. The study was out of bounds when he wasn't there, so to be in that room felt special, like we had secrets to share. He would draw tiny symbols on the pages to mark significant points. A circle with a cross through it would tell me where his crew would be fighting pirates for buried treasure. A tiny bird would signify a helicopter ride to a deserted island. All stories, I realized later, but at the time I was fascinated and completely in awe of him. My father was a true hero at sea. I had no brothers or sisters, so there was no one to burst my young bubble of worship, and all the gifts he brought home were for me. Such was the self-reflective and lonely world of an only child.

The last time he returned from overseas I was eleven years old and not in any way ready to lose my father. I wondered later if he knew it would be his last visit because the gifts he produced were particularly extravagant. He had been all the way to South America and had promised to bring me some golden treasure. I waited in the garden all day, perched on a tree branch so that I could see the village road winding down the hill. I wanted to see his car coming so that I could be at the gate to greet him. I had carved a wooden animal, a seal, that I wanted to give him, and I was so proud of it. It had taken me the whole term to make, much to the exasperation of my woodwork teacher, who had pointed out the many items my classmates had made in the same time. None of their efforts were as polished, detailed, or true to life as mine, though.

At first, it was quite comfortable up there on a wide, leafy spot with the cool spring wind blowing expectation around me. But by the time the sun was directly overhead, my behind had become numb and I was desperately hungry. Still I waited, fidgeting up there in the tree, the occasional bug crawling along my leg or flying across my face, until at last I heard my father's car in the distance, its unmistakable growl coming up the hill towards the house. My heart leapt when I saw the silver-blue bonnet turn the corner, and I jumped down from the tree a little too hastily, hurting my ankle when I landed. Hobbling towards the garden gate, I had just enough time to retrieve the wooden seal from its hiding place near the bird bath before standing on the pathway ready to see my father for the first time in months.

"My bonnie boy," he said and held me tight.

"Dad, I made you a seal." I thrust the wooden ornament into his giant hands.

"Oh it's great, absolutely incredible," he said and held it up to the light so that he could examine all the detail.

We walked hand in hand up to the house in silence. He was a man of few words, but what he did say mattered. My father opened the front door slowly and stood on the doormat for a second. "How is your mother?" he asked.

I couldn't answer. I didn't know what to say, just looked up at him and then at my feet. He nodded and shut the door behind him. He put his suitcase at the foot of the stair and pulled me close, held my cheek in his hand.

"Let's have a look at you," he said. "My, you're growing fast."

⟫•⟪

The golden treasure that my father had promised to bring back from South America was presented to me in the form of an egg. He told me that it was a magic egg; a rare find from the depths of the Venezuelan jungle, said to be laid by ancestors of the ancient dinosaur, the Pteranodon. I wholly believed this story and was so excited by the gift I could hardly touch it, my fingers shaking as he held it out for me in his palm. It was small but perfect, shining with unknown places and with the promise that everything was going to be all right. I immediately ran to get my atlas so that he could show me exactly where he had found it, and we pored over the pages in his study on our matching leather chairs.

"There's something else," he said. He rolled up his shirtsleeve and took off his watch, of silver metal with a blue-and-red striped strap. "I want you to have it."

I took the watch, so overwhelmed at the gesture that I couldn't speak. He put it on my skinny wrist, pulling it tight. Our heads touched together, the smell of pipe tobacco on his breath comforting me.

During his time at home, I clung to him, spent every moment I could by his side. He must have spent time with my mother, but I have no recollection of her being anywhere other than in the shadows. When he left only three weeks later, I was distraught. I felt protected when my father was home, safe in the knowledge that he wouldn't allow what I called "happenings" to rear up and hurt me. But when he was gone, the happenings occurred; they could be unexpectedly frequent, or few and intense, but never non-existent. I lived in terror when my father was away at sea.

That night I put the golden egg under my pillow and hoped it would act as a protective presence, prayed that my special gift had magical powers like my father had told me. I screwed my eyes shut tight and hoped that my mother would stay away, although I knew deep down that this wouldn't happen for long. I wore my father's watch, slept with it close to my face so that I could hear its soft ticking. I whispered to him, over and over, "Come back soon." Every creak on the stair and every shifting shadow from the bright moonlight dancing ominously through clouds made my heart beat faster.

I knew. The ritual would not really work; the egg had no power. My mother would explode that night, or tomorrow, or the next day. She was unpredictable and that would never stop.

———◆———

When my mother was just herself, she was quiet, almost delicate in her ways as she flitted around the house. She would bake cakes and open the pink-and-green patterned curtains in the mornings and go about a routine day like any other normal person. We would have breakfast, lunch, and a cooked dinner, sitting at the small kitchen table together, mostly in silence. I never really enjoyed her even when she was like that, because I was always waiting for normality to disappear and for one of her other moods to torment me. I tried reading a book at the table to try and blank her out, but she would always remain, a silent figure ready to change into someone else. I kept quiet, tried to be small and out of her way so that she was less likely to be riled. Most of the time it was as if she didn't notice I was there and somehow that suited me just fine.

Some days, her lazy, rebellious side came out, and she would spend all day in her pyjamas, watching television. Any of my calls for help or hunger would be met with, "Why should I do anything for you?" I didn't get fed, sometimes for days. I would have to make do with cereal or stale bread and sometimes stolen fruit from the market. At school I would beg for leftovers from other children's lunch boxes, too hungry to be proud. At times like that, my mother would stink of body odour, too idle to wash, her pungent smell filling the room. I simply kept out of her way. These were not the times I really feared. What I dreaded were the loud days, when the "happenings" took over. She often went to the angry place after my father left for a trip, and as I was the only person around, she would direct her anger at me. The duration of these episodes would vary: hours if I was lucky, weeks if I was not. Sometimes they all blurred together. For years I suffered until my existence became normal for me, my fear a manageable emotion. I didn't know any differently.

One day my mother crossed the line and finally awakened a realization in me that my life didn't have to be that way. I was eleven years old after all, more socially aware than I had ever been, and I was exhausted, so tired of it. It was the day the telegram arrived from the Royal Navy Surface Fleet headquarters, to inform her of my father's death whilst in service. The postman arrived early in the morning before school started, so I was still eating my breakfast, being careful to chew quietly and not spill any crumbs on the floor. The transformation to her darker side was instant, as though someone pulled a blind down and released it again to reveal a completely different person. Her face went dark, her hands trembled, and as I watched that terrifying persona was reborn.

"Your daddy's dead, and it's all your fault, you stupid fucking waste of a boy."

I dropped the plate of toast I was holding and made for the

Nondescript Rambunctious

door. She darted across and flattened herself against it. I could have sworn that she somehow grew taller.

"It's your fault and you'll pay for it. It's your fault."

"I didn't do anything," I cried and slumped down on the hallway floor, terrified, my knees weakened by fear.

"Your daddy's dead, he's gone. He didn't want to come back and see your pitiful face again, always crying, always whining."

"Let me out, I've got to go to school." I grabbed my satchel and my coat and tried to get around the side of her.

Her abuse was never physical, more a psychological attack on how I behaved and ultimately how I perceived myself. She ground me down. But this time, she pushed and I went skidding across the kitchen floor and smashed my head against the handle of the cupboard underneath the sink. It hurt so much that I went dizzy, dropped my bag. When she came at me again, I managed to dodge her and fled out of the door. I staggered up the garden path, to the end of our road and didn't stop walking until I had reached the depths of Edinburgh city, surrounded by enough people and noise to numb my fear. I fell into a doorway on Leith Walk, huddled into a corner, and didn't move all night. I must have slept a little because suddenly it was early morning, cars starting to busy the road. Someone had thrown a few coins at me in the night, and they were resting on my leg. Shivering and aching, I managed to get up and stretched a little, the pain in my side shooting through me. Maybe the coins would amount to a hot drink, maybe not. I didn't know what would happen next, but at least I wasn't home.

After two nights of living on the street, it hit me hard that my father was dead. I was begging on the stair leading down to Waverley Station, light rain soaking me to the core, young enough to be getting sympathy looks and notes in my plastic cup. I saw a boy about my age walking along with his dad, looking up at him, telling him something that excited him. The father put his hand on the boy's head, rubbed his hair, and smiled. I started to cry, my tears mingling with the rain and washing away to nowhere. I thought of my father, arriving at the garden gate wearing his uniform and white hat, handsome and strong, my hero. I longed for the golden egg, the atlas, any one of the treasured gifts he had given to me over the years. It would have his fingerprints, his thoughts; it would be a part of him. But I had left everything behind in my haste to get away from home.

As I bent down to pick up some money from the floor, someone tapped on my shoulder.

"How old are you, son?"

I looked up and saw a man with a kind face. He was holding out a hot sausage roll, dripping with ketchup.

"Eleven." I was too tired to think about lying and too hungry to refuse food.

"Then you'd best come with me. This isn't the best place for a wee laddie now, is it?" He took off his coat, padded with a hood, and draped it over my shoulders.

I ate the roll fast. It was the best meal I'd had in days. I walked with him out of the station entrance while some bagpipers started up on the corner of Princes Street. The sun came out for a few seconds and cast a light on the castle, majestic in the background. I rubbed at my arms and felt the watch, tight on my wrist. His watch. I felt warm through, that there was hope for me to be happy.

I spent the next seven years in care.

CHAPTER TWENTY-FIVE

Lizzy Blows Chunks

Uncle Brian left and even I didn't see it coming. He said cheerio in the morning, just like he usually did, all awkward and a wee bit huffy. The boys waved from the window in the living room, and Auntie Maureen didn't look up from the kitchen sink where she was getting their breakfast ready. Like I said, it was just like normal. I was feeling a bit woolly; I had a headache from too many snifters and Tennent's Supers the night before, and I was trying to hide away in the cool of the fridge, pretending to be getting a juice. I liked to think that I said goodbye to Uncle Brian because he never came back that night. I think I did, and if I didn't, then I definitely waved. One of his pals from work came with a letter for Auntie Maureen, and after she read it, she ripped it up into millions of pieces, threw them all in the bin, and didn't speak for the rest of the night. That part was unusual for her, right enough.

"What's going on?" I sat beside her on the sofa when the boys were all in their bed. "Are you all right?"

"Uncle Brian's left us," she said.

"Where's he gone?"

She slumped back and looked at the ceiling. "He says he doesn't love me and that he'll get back in touch with the boys when he's found somewhere else to live."

"What a bastard," I said. "He could have told you to your face."

"Watch your language," she said, then marched off to her bed.

I tried to be nice, to be there for her, but she didn't want to know. I heard her crying and crying until I couldn't stand to listen to it anymore. I crept out of the house to go to Simon's for a bevvy to calm down. It felt like everything was falling apart, that everyone would eventually disappear until I was left on my own in someone else's house at someone else's kitchen table. First Granny Mac, then Dad, then Mum, and now Uncle Brian. If I couldn't rely on my own family to stick around, then I'd have to stick to my friends, to Simon. I kept meaning to go round and see Molly, or at least try and meet her at Maccy D's or something, because her mum still hated me. But the weeks drifted by. I didn't know where they went, most of them spent with Simon. It was better at Simon's anyway; at least we could have a drink and a smoke and a wee snifter if Roy was feeling generous.

It was dead windy out that night. It was rattling at the windows, so there was no way Auntie Maureen could hear me slip out the door. I chucked on Uncle Brian's old wool coat: I'd fancied it for a while and he'd forgotten to take it with him, so it was tough shit for him. It was dead warm and so long that it almost trailed along the ground, how cool was that. I liked the way my Doc Martens stuck out at the front. It smelled of Uncle Brian, mind, his fags and Brut aftershave, but it didn't really bother me. It kind of reminded me of my dad.

When I got to Simon's, I could hear Roy shouting his head off. I opened up the letter box and looked in; couldn't see anything but I could hear that he was totally doing his melt.

"What the fuck, you fucking wee gobshite. Do as you're fucking told. Your Mammy wants more voddy, so go and get some, you fucking wee cunt-fuck, who do you think you are."

"I've no cash," I could hear Simon saying over and over between all the swearing.

"Fucking nick the bastard voddy then. Are you stupid or something, get to fuck, I'll no give you any cash, you fucking wee shite."

I waited outside, behind the hedge of next door's garden. The front door opened and Roy pushed Simon out of the house, shouting after him that he was a cunt-fuck and other things as well. I heard Simon grunt on the floor and pick himself up, muttering something. I peered through the hedge and saw him standing there, glaring at the front door, slammed shut again by Roy. He wasn't wearing his coat and he shivered a bit.

"Hey, cunt-fuck," I whispered through the leaves..

He grinned and came out onto the pavement. "Did you hear that?" he said. "What an arse."

"I'll help you nick some voddy if you like," I said.

"What are you doing here, anyway?"

I told him about Uncle Brian doing a runner and that I couldn't stand being at Auntie Maureen's anymore. He put his arm around my shoulders, dead protective, and said it would be all right. Simon was so cool like that. He'd just been kicked out of his house by his mum's schemie boyfriend, sent to nick her some booze, but he'd always listen to what was on my mind. Like he didn't have any worries of his own. Nothing seemed to get to him, not like it did to me.

We ended up with two big bottles of voddy because it turned out so easy to nick stuff from the offy. I couldn't think why we hadn't tried it before. I went in first and tried to buy a bottle of Strongbow. The guy who works there spent ages asking me how old I was; could he see some ID and all that. Simon wore my coat and hid the bottles in the pockets; walked out just as I'd got out my library card for a laugh. It had a picture of Madonna on it; fuck, what do I want with the library anyway? It wasn't like I did any homework in there or even read any of the shite chick-lit like the books Auntie Maureen borrowed. We decided to drink one of the bottles before we went back to Roy, and went down to our spot at the river. We knew if we took them both back, Roy would take them off us anyway, so what was the point.

The long grasses at the river shielded us from the wind, and it was kind of cosy sat there in the dark. The moon was out and lit up the water, made it look magic. I didn't say anything about it to Simon, in case he thought I was soft or something. He was looking at it as well, though; I could tell. Maybe he was thinking the same thing as me. I wondered how many people got on with their lives without ever saying what they were really thinking about because they thought they'd sound stupid.

We took turns to swig at the bottle, drinking quickly because we didn't have much time. Roy would be pacing up and down, waiting for Simon to get back, and his mum would probably be whining like a sick cat. I could feel the drink burning my throat and then my stomach, but I didn't care, I just kept tipping the bottle and chugging it. Simon snogged me a couple of times and his tongue felt all hot; it was great mixed in with the fire of the booze. We drank so quick that I didn't notice how pished I was getting, and when the bottle was empty, I could hardly walk. Simon wrapped himself around my left side and half-carried me all the way back to his place. I was crying by that time, I wasn't really sure what about particularly, but I just felt sad about everything. He took me inside and laid me down on the sofa in their living room. I heard him stomping up the stair to give his mum her precious voddy and Roy shouting something obscene from the kitchen.

Then I must have blacked out because suddenly it was morning. You could tell the summer was over because the mornings were starting off a bit dark. The curtains in Simon's living room were open, but it wasn't sunlight that woke me up, it was the birds singing and the bin men clarting about outside. At first I didn't know where I was. I sat up and my head pounded like someone had bashed at it with a mallet. There was a terrible smell of sick, and when I put my hands up to cover my nose, I realized that it was mine. I had dried puke on my chin, down Uncle Brian's coat, and there was a pile of it on the carpet underneath the place where my head must have been. It was gross. I sat dead still for a minute, taking it all in and listening for noise, but it was way too early for any of those guys to be up and about. I staggered into the kitchen, trying to be quiet, and found a scabby old J-cloth and a bucket to clean up the sick. I wiped at my face and coat first, the smell making me heave, and I thought I was going to throw up again but managed not to. The puke had wedged itself into the pile of the carpet in places, but I got most of it out and the rest just blended in with the seventies brown pattern.

I poured everything out into the downstairs toilet and put the cloth in the bin. I thought about drinking some water before I left, but my stomach had that feeling that if anything went near it there would be trouble. I paused for a second near the front door, wondering if Roy or his mum had seen me there, if Simon had known I was sick on the floor, what would happen today. Then I opened the door and went out into the cold.

Two bin men whistled at me on my way home. I don't know why. I must have looked like a tramp, nothing to be whistled at. I wanted to run, to get back to Auntie Maureen's in case she was worried about me, but my head was so sore that I could only walk slowly, taking deep breaths. The wind blew through my hair, so cold but not enough to numb the pain.

I was dreading getting back, expecting a full skelping for being out all night, but I was met with complete silence at Auntie Maureen's. I crept up the stair, keeping Uncle Brian's stinking coat on so I could get to my room without making any noise. I saw that the door to Billy's room was open. I didn't even need to look in the room; I could hear his little snores and snuffles. They were all asleep. It seemed no one had even noticed I was gone. I chucked the coat and the rest of my clothes on the floor, pulled on my jammies, and got in bed.

I'd got away with it. That was a good thing, wasn't it?

Was it because of me that everyone had left? Was it something I'd done or how I was? Would Auntie Maureen be gone by morning? I knew that if Mum or Granny Mac were around, they'd tell me straight to my face, so they would. Granny Mac would have said I was a wee besom, a drunk, and a disgrace. Mum would have told me not to take drugs, not to cut myself on my arm, not to hang out with "that" family. And I would have liked it better than getting away with stuff because it would have meant that they cared. I knew it. No one else gave a shit, not even my own dad. Mum would have sat me down at the kitchen table, made me a cup of tea, and put down a plate of chocolate digestives. You need to go to school, she'd have said, make something of yourself. I would have scowled at her. I could just see Granny Mac reaching into her wee clasp bag for a minty lump, rustling at the plastic wrapper, and smiling, despite the face on me. "Want one, my wee darling?"

I just wanted my mum back; I'd never missed anyone so much. I couldn't stand not knowing what happened to her, and I thought about it every day even though I didn't talk about it anymore. I kind of knew she was dead, but because the police had never found her, there was always that doubt in the back of my mind. Simon told me I needed to move on and I knew he was right, but I couldn't help what I felt. It wouldn't ever change.

—⬦—

I met Molly in the street, hadn't seen her for days. She was looking at the CDs in the window of Woolies, standing on her own, twiddling her hair. I'd known her forever, but she was a total stranger at the same time. We hadn't hung out properly for ages, and I felt a bit nervous about saying hello to her for some reason. She looked at me like I was weird or something and even stood back a bit.

"Back to school, then?" I asked, a bit stupid really, seeing as she was wearing her uniform and carrying a new school bag. It was one of those rucksacks made of canvas, and she'd stuck a few badges on it of bands and that, but none that I was into. One said I ♥ McFly.

"Aye," she said. "Not like you, eh? Do they not chase you up about it anymore?"

"It's just not for me, that's all," I said. "And Auntie Maureen couldn't care less what I do."

I smiled but she didn't smile back, just looked at me with a blank expression, like she didn't understand what I'd just said. "Mrs. Jefferson took register, then asked me where you were. I said I had no idea, and for once that was true," she said. "What are you doing with yourself, Lizzy?"

"Uncle Brian left us," I blurted out.

She looked at her feet and said she was sorry, then asked if I wanted to go for a Coke in Maccy D's or something. She'd got a new MP3 player for her birthday and wanted to let me have a listen. It was getting cold to be standing on the street, right enough. I was on my way to Simon's, though, and was already a wee bit late. I said maybe next time, and she looked a bit upset but what could I do? I just wanted to be with Simon; he was the only one who really got me. I felt sorry that we weren't close anymore, but I just couldn't help what I was feeling. She just seemed so much younger than me, with her long socks and hair pulled back in a ponytail and her new toys. I told myself I'd make more of an effort the next week; maybe meet her after school one day.

"Lizzy, do you mind that pact we made that time?" Molly scuffed her shoes on the pavement.

"What do you mean?"

"If we turned thirteen and went a bit mental, we'd tell each other?"

"Do you think I'm mental now, as well? You're just like everyone else, so you are."

She grabbed at my wrist, turned it over so my scratches showed.

"What's all that then?"

"Fuck off, Molly." I pulled away and stormed off. Cheeky cow. She just didn't get what I was going through, still in her perfect world with both her parents and her brother and everything.

I looked back. She was walking off in the direction of home. She had smelled of Hubba Bubba. Bubble gum was for kids. Simon smelled of guys' deodorant, and cigarette smoke with a hint of dope mixed in. I loved that.

CHAPTER TWENTY-SIX

Oliver Plants a Seed

I finally spoke to that scab of a man. He was sitting on a mildew-covered bench on the High Street, smoking and staring. Wasting time. The bench was opposite the electrics shop and there was a television in the window showing a cricket match. He was watching it, although probably didn't understand cricket and couldn't even see the scores properly from there. There was no sign of Lizzy or her friend, and I presumed he had sent them on one of his errands to pick up drugs, money, or whatever else he exploited them with. Often they were dragging their feet behind him, but this time he was alone. He was shaking his leg up and down impatiently as if he was far too busy and important to be waiting for anything. I ripped the handle of my shopping bag, and it dropped to the ground right in front of him. Cans of soup and packets of pasta rolled onto the pavement, and I bent to pick them up.

"They don't make placcy bags like they used to, eh?" He snorted and stumped out his cigarette on the floor next to my hand. A trace of ash landed on my glove and made a smudge on the brown leather.

"They certainly don't. There's nothing that heavy in here," I said quietly and sat down on the bench next to him to tie up the sides of the bag. I tried to ignore the smudge, but I could feel it through the glove, burning.

He looked off into the distance, uninterested, and rubbed his hands together even though it wasn't cold. I noticed that his fingernails were completely black and the skin around them was bitten raw. The undersides of his fingers were rough and yellow. I got a bad taste in my mouth. His pager made a buzzing noise and he left it on his belt, tilting it so he could see the message. He nodded, like something good had happened. I could only imagine what.

"Can I ask you a question?" I said.

"You a fucking copper or something?" he growled and stared at the side of my head.

I didn't move. "No."

"I'm not bothering no one sat here. I'm just minding my own, so don't start with me. Fucking polis, what the fuck," he said and pulled out another cigarette.

"I'm not a policeman, far from it."

"Well, you'd better not be."

"Know where I can get any good gear? I'm new around here."

"Fuck off, what you asking me for, you fucking posh tit?" He paused. "You think I'm some dealer do you as I've no fucking jacket and polished shoes like yous got, get to fuck." He jabbed his cigarette in the air towards my face. Some smoke wafted around me. I could feel it seeping into my clothes, my skin.

An elderly couple walking past stopped in their tracks momentarily to stare. The woman tutted and shook her head.

I managed to remain calm, saying nothing until they were on their way again. "Well, if you hear of anyone let me know. I'm at 16 Fettes Drive. It's the white cottage."

I stood up and left promptly before he could give me any more abuse. I heard him muttering to himself as I walked away, between sharp intakes of breath as he sucked on a cigarette to drive as much nicotine into his system as he could. He was a disgusting specimen of a man and even worse close up. There were grey lines around the neck of his T-shirt and sweat stains under his arms. He stank.

I had to walk past the chip shop. It seemed so popular in the town for some reason. Dirty white tables adorned with paper tablecloths, with red plastic ketchup bottles for squeezing and sharing. Worse still, people taking food home, fat seeping through newspaper, then no doubt dripping down their chins. It was a revolting concept. The only time I'd ventured inside was out of necessity, for Lauren, but the smell of it all had disgusted me: vinegar, battered fish, and fat fryers. How could it be so compelling to so many? I never understood.

That boy was standing in the doorway, his heavy frame almost touching the sides. He was mentally disabled in some way, unable to do anything much but drift in his father's shop. He was staring at me; of this I was quite sure. I could sense his eyes following me down the street. As I passed, he lifted one arm slowly, and pointed at me. He said nothing, just stood silent. I didn't look at him directly, but increased my pace, arms wrapped around my broken bag of groceries. In his insular, extra-sensory world, could he know of my desires, my inner sanctum of depravity? I knew it couldn't be true, that I was over-thinking, but still: it was an unnerving experience. To be noticed.

I went straight home and undressed in the hallway, threw my clothes into the washing machine, and got into a hot shower. Germs and ash and even the indirect run-in with the chip-shop boy had plenty of time to work their way deep into my system, clawing away at my insides. I used the pumice stone on my face, my neck, and torso and didn't stop rubbing until blood mixed with the hot water and swirled down the drain. It was worth the ordeal, just to have planted a tiny seed of potential into Roy's dense skull. He was no doubt sitting on a crumb-covered sofa, drinking his Special Brew, and wondering if I could be a good client of his. And now he knew where I lived. I gave him three days of pondering, and he'd be tapping on my front door like a rat sniffing out a sack of leftovers. And he wouldn't tell anyone he was coming. It couldn't be more perfect.

CHAPTER TWENTY-SEVEN

Lizzy Does the Drop

I was on my way to Simon's. A couple of old farts stared at me from across the street, which I was used to by then. I didn't know if it was my hair, my makeup, or my clothes old folk didn't like. Maybe it was just me. I wondered what it would be like to live in a big city, where everyone was a bit different and nobody cared what you looked like. I just ignored the two of them anyway, even though I was tempted to flick the finger.

Simon's neighbour was outside his house trimming his hedge. He was just a wee guy and the garden gloves made his hands look too big for the rest of him. "I wouldn't go in there the now," he said.

"How?"

"There's been an awful noise, shouting and bawling."

I listened hard and right enough; I could make out Roy going off and Simon's mum crying. I just stood there for a minute, not knowing what to do.

"How old are you when trimming bushes and clipping things off them is something you like doing?"

"Dinnae be cheeky," he said, but grinned. "Away you go and have a wee walk. Come back later, that's what I'd do, darlin'."

I hesitated. I knew he was right but I wanted to see Simon so badly. "It'll be fine," I said.

"Suit yourself." He carried on clipping things with a pincer thing. All the bits were going everywhere; there were some on his hat.

I put my ear to the front door and listened again. When the shouting stopped for a minute, I rang the bell.

"Who the fuck's that," I heard Roy mutter as he opened up.

"Is Simon in?"

"Aye he is, the fuckin' wee skank. He's away up in his room hiding away like a fuckin' tit while his skank of a mother gives me the fuckin' arse," he said, and shouted up the stair. "Simon get yourself down here the now. Your piece of arse here has saved you from a skelping again."

I waited in the hallway for Simon to come down, not wanting to get involved in whatever it was Roy and that witch were arguing about. I wasn't going to object to being called a piece of arse; that much was for sure. I couldn't remember the last time I saw Simon's mum; she was away in her bed that often, but suddenly there she was in front of me, swaying against the kitchen doorframe.

"Hi Lizzy. It's Lizzy isn't it? You're a pretty wee thing, so you are. Come to see Simon have you," she slurred.

She stank of booze and fags; her breath was dead rank, like she hadn't brushed her teeth for a week. She'd got about three inches of black roots showing, and the rest of her hair was so dry that in places it had snapped off.

"Cat got your tongue or something, or do you think we're not good enough for you? Not good enough to speak to, are we?" she carried on, blethering about nothing.

I didn't know what to say to her; it really was like the cat had got my tongue, whatever the hell that meant. I just stared.

"Fuck yous." She disappeared into the kitchen again, lit a fag. I heard the lighter click. Simon ran down the stair, his feet thudding in sets of two. It was all I could do to stop myself flinging my arms around him right there and then.

"Let's go out," I said and jabbed a finger at the kitchen, meaning

"I want to get away from your mum and Roy." Just as I did it, Roy came to the doorway and saw me, I nearly died.

"Can't wait to get away, eh? Fuckin' wee Princess so you are, fuckin' think you're something," he said.

Simon grabbed his coat. "Leave it, Roy," he said.

"No, I won't fuckin' leave it. You're all ganging up on me now, you fuckin' lot of shites."

His eyes were nearly rolling back in his head, he was so high, and I could see his hands trembling like anything. I was scared then, for what he might do. He took a couple of steps towards me, bent forward and leered, his skanky breath hot on my face. "I'll knock that out of you right now, you fuckin' wee whore."

I froze but Simon was brilliant, stepped right in front of me and told Roy to shut it. "You lay a finger on her and I'll kill you," he said.

Then everything happened really fast. Roy punched Simon in the face, knocked him over. The back of his head hit my nose and it started bleeding a bit.

"Don't fuckin' threaten me, you skinny wee fuck," he said and staggered back into the kitchen. Simon's mum started crying, not like a quiet weeping like my mum used to do when she was upset, but a wailing sound like a baby.

"Shut up, you fuckin' cow," Roy shouted and dragged Simon by his ear in front of her. "This lad of yours is a fuckin' pain in the arse."

"Stop it!" My heart was going so fast.

"You," he pointed at me. "Get in here now."

I said nothing, just took a couple of steps forward and stood there, blood dripping on the floor. My brain was telling me to run away, but my legs wouldn't work.

"He's staying here with me and you're going out on a drop-off on your own. How do you like that, Princess fuckin' skank?"

I froze. I looked at Simon, who was wincing with pain. Roy

grabbed a small packet from one of the kitchen drawers and chucked it at me.

"Take that to the address written on the label. It's something for a guy I met. Tell him it's a free sample of what he was looking for last week. He'll know what it is. If you're not back in one hour, you'll not see this fuckin' little cunt of a boyfriend. Do you understand me, Princess?"

I nodded and picked up the packet from the floor. It was dead light; hard to believe anything was in there. Simon looked up at me, like he was saying sorry, and I knew I had to take the package or he would be beaten up so badly. As I left the house I could still hear his mum wailing, like she was in pain or something. Fucking pure mad, it was. The guy next door stood up from picking at his lawn and watched me after me as I left.

"You okay, hen? You're bleeding."

I just shrugged and sunk my hands and the package deep into my pockets, made for the address on the label. I knew where it was, one of the cottages right opposite the corner shop where Mum used to work.

It was where Mum used to work. That sounded so final, like she was never going to be there again. I pulled my hood up and cried all the way there. I cried for me and Simon and that drugged-up ned we had to put up with; I cried for Mum and Granny Mac and for Auntie Maureen losing Uncle Brian. I cried because I was angry with my life and because there was nothing I could do about it, absolutely nothing. It was unbelievable how much shite I'd been dealt that year. The wind bit into my face, so cold I thought my tears would freeze on their way down.

When I got to the shop, I was desperate for a fag; Simon usually had a pack on him so I cadged from him. Buying some meant seeing Jessica, but I really couldn't care about anything at that point. I wiped at my face with my sleeve, licked it, and tried to get the dried blood off as best I could. Then I barged in there like nothing had happened. Jessica was in there with Mr. McTavish, so I knew she wouldn't give me loads of bad chat anyway. She couldn't, not with him right there.

"All right, Jessica? I'll have ten Marlboro Lights, please."

"You sixteen?" Mr. McTavish piped up.

"Aye, she's sixteen. I know her," said Jessica.

She wasn't so bad after all. I gave her the money and she passed over the fags, asked if I was okay.

"You're looking dead rough, Lizzy," she said.

"I'm just not sleeping very well at the moment." I tried not to cry again.

"What's that on your nose, did you hurt yourself?"

"No, I just had a nosebleed. It's nothing."

She came round the front of the counter and put her arms around me. It was a strange thing to do, I thought, for her. "You take care of yourself," she said and dabbed at my face with a tissue.

I must have looked worse than I thought. "Thanks, I will."

I stopped in the square outside the shop, found a wee bench, and sat down for a minute to have a smoke. There was easily enough time to get back within the hour, and it gave me a chance to pull myself together. I hadn't done a drop-off on my own before. When I was with Simon, I hardly even thought about it. He was so confident, always knew the right way to approach someone or pass a package over. Knocking on someone's door was different though, a bit easier I thought. You would know you had the right person, right? But there was also something I didn't like about it; maybe it was the fact that I was going to someone's home and not out in some random, exposed place with other people around. I'd be there alone. Still, the thought of Roy back at Simon's was scarier, and if I didn't get on with it, he'd do something really bad. And, if anything happened to me, they would know where I was, where I'd been. I was terrified for Simon more than anything.

So I smoked that fag down to the brown tip, got up, and did it.

I walked up the pathway to the cottage and knocked. I stood back a little, checked to see if I was visible to Jessica, and thankfully I wasn't. She was a nosy cow. The door opened slowly and I held my breath, not knowing who to expect, but it was that tall guy that I'd seen around a bit, the one that wore funny hats and gloves. He stared at me sometimes, but then who didn't? He was actually quite good-looking for an old guy. I was taken aback, but I have to say that he seemed more surprised to see me than I was of him. He looked like he'd seen a ghost or something.

"I've got something for you," I said. "Can I come in?"

There was a bit of a silence, which was dead awkward. I started to wonder if I had the right place.

"Yes, of course, of course." He stepped back and let me in.

We went through to the living room before he spoke again. "Would you like to sit down?" He was dead posh, like someone off the news or something.

"No, I don't think so." I stood in the middle of the room with my arms folded, trying to look tough. There wasn't much in the room to look at, nothing on the walls. It smelled of paint and bleach.

"A drink, perhaps? A juice or a soda?"

"I'm just here to give you something, a package from Roy." I wanted out, quick as possible.

"I'm not sure I know anyone called Roy," he said.

"Are you sure?" Fuck's sake, I was in the wrong place.

"Well, what does he look like?"

Was he playing games or something? He was a bit of an arse. "Like a schemie, like a ned, like someone you might avoid in the street. He's got a mullet with streaks in it, dirty jeans. He's usually off his melt."

"Ah, yes, I know him. There's only one person I've seen around here that fits your excellent description. And this man sent you with his package. Why didn't he come himself?"

"Do you want it, or not?" He was starting to get right on my nerves.

"How much does he want for it?"

"Nothing, he told me it was just a wee sample."

He took it, finally, and gave me ten quid for coming. That was the best bit. I shoved it in my pocket and made for the door quick; he was giving me the creeps. He kept on looking at me funny and pulling at his hair. Well, job done. I could get back to Simon and get him away from Roy.

❖

I'd never seen anyone in such a mess as Simon was at the end of that day. I couldn't remember a lot about Mum when she used to get beaten up, partly because I was shielded from her in the worst parts, I just knew I was. But I hoped she never looked like Simon did after Roy had seen to him.

When I got back to Bannerley Drive, I knew something terrible had happened. For a start, everything was quiet, and at first I thought they might have gone out. Then when I knocked, the door opened slowly and a voice from behind it just said, "In the kitchen."

I was dead scared, my hands were shaking, and I went all sweaty. It was Simon's mum. She floated away up the stair without even looking at me. I didn't want to go in there; I was dreading what I was going to see. It was the quiet that I couldn't stand. I heard a faint noise, a wee murmur, and then I realized that it was Simon in there and at least he was alive.

He was slumped on a chair at the kitchen table, his head resting on one outstretched arm. His face, head, chest, and hands were all covered in blood. The blood was coming from everywhere: his ears, eyes, mouth. His head was split on the right-hand side; blood was oozing out of it and dripping onto the table. I dry heaved, lurched forward. I felt his pain and it hit me hard. I went to him and put my hands on his face, the blood smearing all over my fingers.

"Simon. Can you stand up?"

"I don't know," he whispered.

I grabbed a tea towel, held it on the cut on his head. "We need to get you to hospital, Simon. Can you stand up, can you try?"

"No, I can't," he said.

I heard footsteps then and the door belted open.

"He doesn't need a hospital. He's fine, he's a fuckin' whiner," Roy said, staggering, sweating, reeling towards me.

I cowered behind Simon, even though he wouldn't be able to protect me.

"You did this to him. How could you?"

"You get that wee packet to the posh twat?"

"Aye," I said. "It's done."

"Good. You've got another job to do, the pair of yous, something urgent that I've no got the time to do myself," he said.

"I can't move," said Simon.

"You've really done it this time, haven't you?" I said and then regretted opening my mouth again. Roy went off on one, started kicking at the air and swaying.

"He fucking deserved what he got, so shut it. The job can't wait. Simon. If you won't go with the fucking Princess here, then she'll have to go by herself again, tough fucking shite."

"What is it, I'll go," I said. I thought it best to go along with what he wanted; he was totally off his melt and dangerous.

"It's important, very important. Get yourself from Inverness to Edinburgh Waverley and then meet a guy on Platform Two by seven the night. He won't wait and if you're late there'll be big trouble. This mess is nothing compared with what I'll fuckin' do if you fuck this one up, and this time it'll be to the pair of yous two fucking wee shites."

He sniffed long and hard and his eyes were big, staring. Simon groaned and tried to stand up. I stood close to him and he put some of his weight on my shoulder. I felt some warm blood splash on my cheek. It was Simon's blood though, so I didn't mind and let it trickle down the side of my face. I knew I had to get him out of there even if I had to carry him. He took a couple of steps forward, testing his legs.

"Give Lizzy the pack or whatever it is we're taking and then we'll go." Simon was blinking quickly to stop the blood from dripping into his eyes.

Roy leered at us, grabbed a large pack from behind him, and held it out for me to take.

"Get this to Waverley for seven or I'll fuckin' batter yous both," he said and disappeared up the stair.

"I'm going with you," said Simon.

"Too fucking right you are. I'm not leaving you with that monster," I said.

I chucked the pack in my duffel bag and helped Simon on with his coat, held the tea towel to his head again. I had to make a decision of what to do, and fast. There wasn't time to get him to the hospital. It was a drive away and I didn't want to call an ambulance or ask Auntie Maureen to take us. She'd freak and probably call the police. We'd have to go to Molly's; it wasn't too far to walk and her mum used to be a nurse or a care worker or something. I thought she'd know what to do anyway. She hated us, but that was the last of my worries. I'd known her for a long time and she was nice underneath it all.

We got out of that fucking stinking house, but it was slow going. Simon was in so much pain; it hurt him to walk, talk, and even to breathe properly.

"Simon, I'm taking you to Molly's place. Get you cleaned up," I said and half-pulled him up the curb on the other side of the road.

He groaned. "Don't say nothing, Lizzy."

"I won't," I said, "but I'll have to tell her something."

We walked in silence, both concentrating on moving without falling over, both scared and hurting and wondering what would happen next. When we got to Molly's house, Simon was in agony; I thought he was going to start crying. The bleeding just didn't want to stop, and I was covered in it as well. We gave Molly's mum a terrible fright when she saw us; she thought I was hurt as well, I was that messed up.

"Jesus, what happened to you?" She ushered us into the house. She looked at Simon a bit suspicious at first. He hadn't exactly been flavour of the month with Molly and her family, and he looked well dodgy most of the time, and that was without the blood on him. The hair, the tattoos, the clothes, and that mess. I didn't really blame her.

"Simon got beaten up and I wondered if you could help him. I'm sorry but you're nearer than Auntie Maureen's, and I didn't know where else to go, I'm sorry," I said, rambling.

She grabbed the phone, held on to it. "And did this person hurt you as well, Lizzy?"

"No, I'm all right," I said. "Can you help Simon, though? Just until we can get to the hospital?"

"I should call the police," she said, still holding the phone.

"Please don't. It'll make everything so much worse." I was panicking a bit then. "I promise we'll go to the hospital and check him out properly. We just need the bleeding to stop the now."

And then she did it, bless her heart; she did a good job as well. She even had Simon smiling as she bandaged and iced and put wee plasters that look like butterfly stitches on his head. She didn't ask any more questions, but she kept looking over at me and humming a wee tune. I didn't know what it was, but it was nice.

I went and washed myself up a bit in the bathroom. She said I could use one of their spare towels in the airing cupboard. It was dead warm in there, little soaps shaped like shells in a wee saucer, everything clean and shiny. Mum used to like those wee shell soaps too, the purple ones that smelled of lavender. I stared at myself in the cabinet mirror. I looked terrible, encrusted blood on my cheeks and in my hair. My eyeliner had smudged down one side of my face so it looked like I'd got a shiner. I used toilet roll to wash it off and dabbed at the blood in my hair as best I could without getting bits of paper stuck in it. I grabbed a green towel out of the cupboard and held it against my face. It was soft and warm and I didn't want to let it go.

Simon couldn't face anything, but me and Molly's mum had a cup of tea and some chocolate digestives to dunk in. Even though I knew there was the job for Roy to get on with, I felt safe for a bit, sitting in Molly's house with the clock ticking on the mantel. Someone else's home.

"Molly will be back from school for lunch today. Will you wait around for her? She'd be so glad to see you, Lizzy. She really misses you," she said.

"I miss her too," I said, and realized that it was true. "But I should get Simon checked out first, you know? I could come over tomorrow and play some CDs or something, what do you think?"

"I think that would be good," she said and smiled at me again with a look on her face that said she didn't really believe me. "And how are you getting on at your Auntie Maureen's? Molly said that Brian has left. It can't be easy for you all."

Typical Molly, gobshite of the year.

"I think she's better off without him, but it isn't easy, right enough," I said. "What with all those wee boys and me as well."

"I'm sure you're a big help to her. You girls are good to have around," she said. She held Simon's face in her hands and looked at him right in the eyes. "Look after my Lizzy and try and stay out of trouble, you."

CHAPTER TWENTY-EIGHT

Oliver and the Arrival

I was in utter torment after Lizzy appeared on my doorstep. So young but carrying a worldly experience beyond her years, vulnerable yet defiant; she was an absolute vision. As I'd stopped watching the newsagents quite so avidly, I was unaware she was in the immediate vicinity, let alone outside my house. I was taken so completely by surprise to see her right there in front of me. She was the last person I expected to visit, and her tentative knock on the door I put down to beautiful fate.

Of course I had been following her progression, or rather her degeneration, since her mother left the world. But my observations were always from a certain distance, and even if I managed to manipulate a close vantage point, I had to hide behind a book or slide low in my seat. It was a pleasure to see her up close and focusing her attentions on me without my having to make any effort of nonchalance. There she was on my doorstep, black-rimmed eyes and young, white skin, but two feet away.

I asked her inside and she stepped boldly through to the living room, her outsized coat trailing along the floor. My blood pumped fast. I could feel it throbbing through my body at the very thought of her innocence. She had come to my home alone, so pitifully unaware of the magnitude of it. I found it at once endearing and arousing, a new experience for me. She had developed into a teenager that summer; her breasts had grown along with her attitude. I could smell cigarette smoke and some kind of cloying cologne, but for some reason it didn't repulse me, only served to strengthen her status as a raw but innocent young girl.

Roy had sent her with the sample. What kind of person sends a child to deliver drugs?

I gave her a ten-pound note for her trouble, which she accepted graciously; her fingertips touched mine in the transaction. The contact sent shivers through me, and my scalp tingled, hairs on end. I felt a desperate desire to have her naked in the basement, but resisted temptation. Roy at least must have known where she was; I would be an instant suspect if she disappeared. Someone could have seen her at the door, too. I reluctantly let her leave my house, but afterwards her shadow continued to occupy my thoughts. A woman and her daughter, one after the other, was a fantastic and immensely desirable idea. It was also a dangerous one and something that would create a great deal more suspicion. Sometimes temptation, however, could all too easily override my sensibilities. What to do?

That night I flushed the dirty drugs down the toilet before cleansing my body and my mind in the hope that I might be set free from that perilous ideal of a mother-daughter abduction. Scalding water, my medical soap, and a tough pumice stone slowly scraped the contamination away from my skin, my bones, and scalp. I took care to give all parts of my body equal attention and emerged from the bathroom pink, glowing, and in some areas, bleeding. It felt good, like something terrible had been removed, seeped out into the atmosphere never to be seen again. In its place was an overriding resentment for the man who had put temptation into my path, the man who sent a young girl unaccompanied to my house to deliver his filth. I already had an intense hatred for those who took advantage of children, cowards like Roy who would never stand up to someone equal in strength or sordid mentality.

I went beyond hatred, however, and into the realm of murderous. The feeling came over me the second I stepped out of the shower. It loomed and raged until it overwhelmed me and lodged itself firmly inside. Lizzy needed me just as I needed her, and I made a decision then to rid her of the man who was putting her in such terrible danger. He wouldn't present much of a challenge, but I relished the thought nevertheless. It had been an age since I experimented with a man, and I knew one particularly valued subscriber would love it.

⇒◆⇐

I waited around on the High Street for most of the following afternoon in the hope of seeing Roy. I knew it was pointless going early in the morning as the lazy "ned," as Lizzy called him, didn't tend to get out of bed much before noon. But even he was late coming out. I browsed in shop windows, drank tea in the café, queued in the post office for stamps that I didn't need, and even bought some sweets contaminated with the multiplying germs from that dreadful Woolworths that hadn't changed since the 1970s. They would go straight in the bin. As I came out of there, cringing at the décor, I saw Roy at last sitting on a bench facing me, smoking a cigarette as always and watching the ash fall to the ground.

I took a moment to watch him before I approached the bench. I couldn't let him feel my rage and I took some deep breaths to let some anger out. His foot tapped repeatedly like he was nervous and he scratched at his greasy scalp. I sat down on the opposite end of the bench and pretended to rummage through the contents of my bag, reluctant to sit too close. He continued to look at the ground. I suppose he was accustomed to this kind of thing.

"Thanks for the sample, it wasn't bad," I said under my breath.

"I've plenty more where that came from, you ken?"

He still didn't look at me, just concentrated on his cigarette ash, breathing heavily with that wheeze so common amongst heavy smokers. His stupidity on that front riled me more than ever.

"Bring me fifty quid's worth tonight to start with," I said. "And this time do your own dirty work."

He snorted down the contents of his nose. "What's that supposed to mean?"

"Come yourself, don't send her."

"Why, did my wee girly do something wrong? I'll fuckin' skelp her if she did."

"Not at all. I just have a proposition for you, and I don't want to deal with a child." I walked away fast before he could retaliate. I didn't look back, although I could feel his eyes burning into me. That would give him something to think about.

It was almost dark when I got home. The winter nights were looming and the clocks were about to go back to make the days even shorter. I knew he would come; there was no question. I had offered him money, baited him with the prospect of a larger deal, and finally irritated him with the last word. All I had to do was prepare my strategy and make the sure the basement room was set up for my next experiment. The loyal viewers of NondescriptRambunctious.com were about to get two surprises. First, they would see another body within a year of the last one, and second, they would be looking at a man. I hoped his already sallow skin and sunken flesh would make his departure from this world quick and painful.

I prepared the room, cleaned it with disinfectant and a scrubbing brush; made sure the lights were working and the camera was set up properly. I put out an announcement to my subscribers. They were to watch for the next imminent installment, showing, or experiment, whatever they chose to call it. Helen sent a short note back, expressing her surprise on my choice and congratulating me. She would relish the change in subject to a man. I didn't seek her approval or anyone else's, but it was good to receive it anyway.

I cleansed myself hard then sat quiet for over an hour, sore and glowing.

The minutes dragged.

My wrist flickering, I couldn't help but look at my watch constantly, agitated and itching with anticipation. I drank a small scotch, nibbled on a cracker, but didn't feel hungry.

Finally, at 10:23, there was a knock at the door and I could smell his rancid body odour from where I was sitting. He'd probably been drinking and would want another. I sucked in deep, and rage boiled to the surface once more.

Here was body number nineteen.

CHAPTER TWENTY-NINE

Lizzy's Angel

We stepped out into the cold again and made our way to the bus stop. The number three went all the way to Inverness Station. There was no point hanging about in Dalbegie, so we thought we might as well get going. The bus was dead slow as well; it stopped everywhere. Simon looked a lot better but he didn't say much, just looked at the floor and held onto my hand really hard, like he was scared I was going to do a runner or something. I wouldn't have done that, though. Simon was all I had.

The bus came eventually and we got a seat at the back so no one would stare at us, but it was bumpy back there. Every time we went over a hole in the road, Simon winced and squeezed at my hand tighter than ever. I could tell he was really hurting even though he was still saying nothing. I opened the window just a bit, felt the cold on my face, and hoped the package drop would go smoothly, that whoever we were meeting wasn't a nutter.

When we got to Inverness Station, it was rammed. I plunked Simon on the floor near WHSmith and got in the queue for the tickets. That was one thing I'd say for Roy, he always gave us money for expenses in with the package. There was a couple of fifties stuck onto the parcel by an elastic band, with an unspoken agreement that we'd give him our receipts and change as proof we hadn't done him out of anything. As if we'd dare.

An announcement came on the tannoy, that there were disruptions to all the services, leaves on the line, blah blah. I wasn't really listening. We had plenty of time to get to Edinburgh so I wasn't worried at first, but when a few more trains got cancelled, I started to get really nervous. The ticket guy looked pissed off when I got to the front of the queue.

"Will I get to Edinburgh by seven?" I asked.

"Don't know doll, maybe, maybe not. I'm not David Copperfield," he said and held up his palms like it wasn't his fault.

I must have looked like I was going to cry. I felt like it, right enough.

"Buy your tickets anyway, doll, and if you can't get there, you'll get your money back," he said. "How about that?"

I took the tickets back to Simon and found him covered in pennies where some folk had thought he was a homeless guy.

"Spare any change," he said and grinned at me.

"It's not fucking funny, Simon," I said. "We might not get there on time and then what are we going to do?"

"Sorry. I'm just at the end of it," he said and I knew what he meant. "We could always go back to the guy you took the sample to this morning, sell him the whole pack."

"I'm not going back there again, I tell you that," I said.

Simon sat up straight, all worried. "Why, what did he do?"

"Nothing. He was just a bit creepy, that's all."

He relaxed again, sat and stared at the tickets like they were going to magic us away to Edinburgh.

That guy was fine, quite nice to me really, but I just got a bad feeling about him. Sometimes that happened with me. His house smelled funny, like a dentist or a hospital or something. It was clinical; yeah that's a good word for it, not like a proper home but like somewhere you'd go for an appointment. He didn't have any

Nondescript Rambunctious

photos on his mantelpiece or on his shelves like most folk have, of their family or their dogs or whatever. Mum used to have hundreds of dusty wee frames, of family, me, Granny Mac, the boys. Everyone. He offered me a juice, but I didn't want to hang about so I just said I had to go. I wasn't sure quite what it was, I just wanted to get out of there, and the fact that Roy had anything to do with him wasn't helping.

"Please thank your friend for the sample," he had said when I was back on his doorstep.

"I will do," I said to him. "And if you like it then you can go see him about it."

Let Roy deal with him. They deserved each other.

⇒•◦•⇐

The train eventually left Inverness past five o'clock, so there was no hope of getting to Waverley on time to meet Roy's drop-off. We got on it anyway, just in case this guy we were supposed to be meeting had heard about the delays. It was better than going back straightaway, and we were sick of sitting in the freezing cold waiting room, smoking fags. Even though I'd bought more Marlboro Lights with Roy's money, we were running out of them. We were so bored and stressed out about the trains and Roy and everything that had happened.

It was a free-for-all on the train because so many folk had to get on it. Your seat number meant nothing. Simon and I stomped to the back and grabbed seats in a two, so we didn't have anyone facing us, staring and wondering why Simon was beat up, what we were up to, and why my hair was such a straggling mess with bits of blood tangled up in it.

Simon sat back and shut his eyes, his hand resting on my leg, which felt good. It was like he was putting his hand on what was his. I liked being his. It was already dark, but I sat and looked out the window anyway. Every so often we'd pass a few houses close up, their wee back gardens nearly on the train tracks. Folk that lived in them must have been used to the noise of the trains. Lights on; people having their tea; talking about their days like any other normal family. Maybe they were watching a quiz show on the telly, shouting out the wrong answers, and laughing at each other. The dog's done a smell; Granny needs another cup of tea; Mum wants another jammy piece; oh I shouldn't, I've had three already ... I longed to be in one of those places with the lights on, all warm and friendly, lots of love and just a bit of noise.

My face hit the cold of the window, steam clouding it up. I left it there until I could feel my cheek going a bit numb. Simon was fast asleep; I heard his breathing dead slow and regular. He looked peaceful for once, if you didn't count the bruises and cuts. At least he had some escape before we found out who was or wasn't waiting for us at the other end of the journey. There was no way I was going to sleep. I just had the window and my bitten nails to keep my mind off things.

We stayed like that, Simon asleep with his hand on my leg and me leaning against the glass, until the train chugged into Waverley Station, grey and dark, damp and uninviting. It was 8:42 and we were nearly two hours late. I wondered if we shouldn't just stay on the train and drift back again. No one could hurt us sat there; it was just me and Simon in the quiet. Simon woke up and groaned that he needed to go pee, and he pulled at my hand to help him up. He was stiff from sitting in one position for so long and I had to half-carry him out of the door and onto the platform, everyone busying themselves around us, rushing to wherever they were late getting to. One guy bumped into me with his suitcase and I gave him the finger, not that he noticed.

There was a toilet on the platform so Simon stopped in there and I waited on a wee bench, watching everyone walk by. Edinburgh smelled different to Dalbegie and to Inverness. Granny Mac used to bring me once a year in the summer, and she said the smell had something to do with beer and hops. It always amazed me that so many people lived around a city that smelled like booze. I breathed it in and remembered her, that laugh, that red coat she wore with the big, round buttons. I didn't mean to, but the thought of her made me cry again so when Simon came out of the loo I was bawling. He was dead sweet, sat down next to me and put his arms around me, told me not to worry about anything. It was all going to be all right. I didn't tell him what I was crying about; it would have sounded dead stupid, considering.

"The man's not going to be there," I said.

"I know," he said. "So will we see what's in the package?"

"What?"

"Let's open the pack, Lizzy. Let's just fuckin' open it."

"We can't."

"Aye, we can."

To open one of Roy's packages was like asking for the biggest trouble of your life. He had threatened us with death a few times if we even squeezed at them. The thought of it made me stop my crying and I looked up at him, shook my head.

Simon picked up my bag. "There's no one around. Come into the loo with me and let's look inside it, come on."

"God, Simon. I don't know."

"Come on, it'll be all right," he said and let me through the door.

He sat on the floor in one of the cubicles, which was a bit minging but it was dry and it didn't really smell in there. I sat on the loo seat. He reached into my duffel, got hold of the plastic bag, and carefully took out the package. It was a big one, quite heavy compared to some of the other ones we'd lugged about. He put it on his lap and looked at it for a minute. "Ready?"

"I want to know what it looks like, what it smells like, what the real stuff is. Roy's given us wee tasters but I bet we've had the crap. This'll be the good shit," I said. "Go for it." I was talking brave, but

I didn't feel what I was saying. I just wanted to be strong, to stop crying, for Simon to be proud of me in some way.

Simon started to peel at the packing tape and I just sat and watched, feeling slightly sick. He got the first bit off, then the rest came easily and the brown paper fell open on his lap. We sat and looked at it in silence.

"Fuckin' hell," I said.

Simon looked up at me and grinned. "Looks like this was a bigger job than we thought, eh," he said.

Right in front of us were six piles of fifty quid notes, six fucking piles of them. I'd never seen so much money; there must have been thousands there. I reached down and touched it and my hand was shaking.

An announcement came on the station tannoy then and it made me jump.

"The next train to arrive on Platform Three will be the overnight service to London King's Cross. Passengers can wait on the main concourse until the train is ready for boarding. The next train to arrive on Platform Three will be the overnight service to London King's Cross."

I looked at Simon and he grabbed my hand. "Let's go, Lizzy. We need to get out of here, take the money, and go to London. They'll never find us."

"What about Auntie Maureen?"

"What about her?"

"I don't know, right enough." I thought for a second and knew Simon was right. What about her? She probably wouldn't notice I was gone for a couple of days and then it'd only be because the house was a tip and I wasn't around to clear it up for her. There was nothing left for me in Dalbegie. There was fuck all.

We took some notes for our pockets and wrapped up the package again, put it back into my duffel bag, and pulled the drawstring tight. My heart was going so fast I thought I was going to pass out. We moved around the station like two mad flies, grabbed two meals from Burger King, some cool magazines from WHSmith before it closed, some fags, and cans of juice. I even remembered to stop in Boots and get some Anadin for Simon. By that time, they were letting folk on the platform and we moved our way to the back of the train. We could buy our tickets on board. We had a short wait; Simon had his hood up in case the guy we were supposed to meet had a photo of him or had met him before. We were just paranoid, I suppose. We huddled together, the bag of money between us, shivering a bit, giggling a bit, until we were allowed to get on the train. I'd never felt so happy and excited and nervous all at once.

=◈=

It was the overnight train and we got ourselves a wee sleeper. There was one going spare, so we nabbed it. We paid for it mind, but who cares when you've a bag full of cash? The ticket guy held up our fifty to the light, and I didn't really blame him for being suspicious about us. Simon looked like a junky, right enough. He let us have it, though; said we looked like we needed it.

We sat together on the bottom bunk and had our burgers and a sneaky fag, wafting the smoke towards the window. Simon could hardly eat, his lip was dead swollen, and I could tell he was hurting. I gave him a couple of Anadin and he gulped them down with his Coke. Then he kicked off his trainers, got in the covers, and fell asleep straightaway. It was like he hadn't slept in a week. Roy's beating had pure sapped the life out of him.

I shut the window and hopped up to the top bunk, but I was too excited and scared to sleep. I couldn't stop thinking about what Roy would do when he realized we'd done a runner. He'd swear and kick things and take it out on Simon's mum. Then he'd try and find us, of course he would, but how far would he go? I reckoned at first he'd hunt for us in Inverness and then Edinburgh. By the time he'd combed every inch of those cities, we'd be well away. I'd never been to London, but someone once told me it was ten times the size of Edinburgh. A good place to hide.

The carriage was rocking with the train, and after lying there for a while, I calmed down. My pillow wasn't bad and the cotton sheets smelled of washing powder, clean and comforting. I turned round and lay with my head the other end, so I could see out the window and watch the stars. I wondered if Granny Mac was up there. She'd be dunking a biscuit in her tea and rooting for me. She was the brighter star on the far left of the window, with a lot of space around her. "You go, my darling," she was saying. "You'd have come to nothing if you'd stayed in that place. It's gone down the tubes, that town." Granny Mac always knew what was best. She was amazing, that's what she was.

Near the top of the window there was a dead bright star with a tiny cluster of diamonds around it, and I told myself that was Mum. She'd know I was doing the right thing too. There's no way she'd have let me anywhere near Roy if she'd been around. He was scum. I think she'd be proud of me that I got Simon away from him, rescued him. I saved us both. I could hear her voice now, clear as anything. With the rhythm of the train, she was saying, "You're my wee angel, you're my wee angel," over and over. Her star blurred and my eyes drooped, as the long day and exhaustion crept up on me and pulled me down. As I fell into sleep, I felt her hand for the last time, pressing on my forehead. I thought, Well, now you can watch out for me, Mum. Now you're my angel. She'd be with me wherever I was. As I said before, it's not about the place. It's the people inside that make it.

Nondescript Rambunctious

www.nondescriptrambunctious.com

Username: WatchWithOliver

Password: St@rv@tion18

Backy – piggy-back (someone can also give you a backy on a bike)

Batter – beat up, kick the crap out of someone (different to the batter on a fish, although you could batter someone WITH a fish)

Besom – cheeky woman, a bit of a monkey

Bevvy – alcoholic drink of any description

Blether – talk too much about nothing, inane chat

Blow chunks – vomit, chunder, puke, spew, barf, chuck up, yack

Bogging – disgusting

Braw – beautiful, lovely, awesome

Choob – idiot, stupid person

Dinger – get excited or angry (you can do your dinger, or go your dinger – but never ring your dinger or it'll get awfy sore)

Eeejit – idiot, wally, a right twat

Gobshite – talks a lot of gossip and rubbish

Greetin' – crying

Heid – head

Jammy Piece – a jam sandwich (also a jeely piece or a piece n' jam depending on where you live)

Jobby – poo, turd (this wasn't actually used in the book, but it's such a great word)

Lang may yer lum reek – long may your chimney smoke (I do hope you have a long and prosperous life, old bean)

Lugging – dragging or carrying something heavy

Melt – head, like 'you're doing my head in' or 'he was off his melt'

Minging/Minger – horrible, smelly, skanky, rank

Ned – acronym for Non-Educated Delinquent, a chav, might wear a shell-suit, a baseball cap, and white trainers (optional bum-fluff on the upper lip)

Numpty – moron, twit, pillock

Peely Wally – pale, sickly, wan

Pish – pee

Pished – drunk

Puss – face (whit's wrong wi' yur greetin' puss?)

Schemie – someone living in a housing scheme, a term used mainly on the East Coast and similar to a Ned (but hey, let's not get over-excited about who says what and where)

Skelp – cuff, slap with an open hand, like a skelped arse or lug (you can also skelp down a pint if you like to do that sort of thing)

Snifter – a snorting of drugs in powder form

Skive/Skiver – not doing any work or pretending to do more than you are

About the Author

Jackie Bateman is originally from England and will always champion the Marmite sandwich. She grew up in Kenya, spent her early adult years in the streets of London and the pubs of Edinburgh, and is now settled in beautiful Vancouver with her husband and two children. *Nondescript Rambunctious* is her first novel. She can be found at www.jacbateman.com.

FIRST BOOK COMPETITION

A NOTE ON
THE FIRST BOOK COMPETITION

The national First Book Competition, sponsored by The Writer's Studio at Simon Fraser University to celebrate its 10th anniversary, was a first in Canada. It was a response to the ever increasing difficulty new or emerging writers face in trying to get their work published. Contest organizers received 200+ submissions, coming from Canadian writers as far away as Italy and New Zealand. Partnering publisher, Anvil Press, agreed to publish the three winning entries in the genres of creative non-fiction, fiction, and poetry.

The three First Book Competition winners are all Canadian writers, writing in English, who have not previously published a book. They submitted original, book-length manuscripts to the competition.

The winners are: Myrl Coulter of Edmonton, Alberta for *The House with the Broken Two* (Creative Nonfiction), Jackie Bateman of Vancouver for *Nondescript Rambunctious* (Fiction), and Rachel Thompson of Vancouver for *Galaxy* (Poetry).

The Writer's Studio is a one-year, continuing studies creative writing certificate program at Simon Fraser University.

For more information visit: www.thewritersstudio.ca.